D1398953

A

Daughters

Rage

A Novel by

Roni J.

Roni J.

This is a work of fiction. All of the characters, organizations, and events portrayed in this novel are either products of the author's imagination or are used fictitiously. Any resemblance to actual persons, living or dead is purely coincidental.

© 2013 Sharonna Jones Baltimore, MD

All rights reserved. No part of this book may be reproduced or transmitted in any form without written permission from the author. With exception to reviewers, magazine articles, newspaper, and radio host who have permission who may quote brief passages for public display.

A Daughters Rage

Acknowledgements

First I want to thank My LORD and Savior for allowing me to breathe and blessing me with my talent to write. I want to give a Big THANK YOU to Fanita "Moon" Pendleton, Rasheed Carter and David Weaver for giving me the opportunity to show the world my gift. My friend's Toya, Geraldo, Kevin and Nette for being there for me when my back was against the wall. I also want to

thank a special man in my life that's been there for me at my lowest and still is to this day. Giving me words of encouragement and motivation. When I first told you I was writing a book all you said was "Go for it. You can do it!" You know who

you are.

A Special shout out to my kid's T'ajai, Da'shawn and Antijuan. Mommy loves you with all of my being. I'm doing this for you! And to my mom Wanda O'cain I appreciate you doing all that you do and I love you. To the man who has spent the last 16 years being my dad Mr. Stevie O'cain Thank you. And my birth father Andre Jones

Roni J.

though we hardly ever agree I love you. If I was told this time last year that I would be writing my first book I wouldn't have believed it. To anyone who has a dream know that you can achieve it. Believe it and it can happen. Shout out to my BDP sisters! Last but not least MY TEAM, MY FAM, BDP AND TEAM BANKROLL SQUAD!

"IT'S NOT A GANG! IT'S A LIFESTYLE!"

A

Daughters

Rage

A Novel by

Roni J.

Roni J.

A Daughters Rage

Prologue

It felt like a freezer outside but I didn't care; my favorite football team the Baltimore Ravens had won the Super Bowl last night and I was there to see it all along with my daddy. It was a night I would never forget. I was running through the house singing, "We are the Champions," still pumped up from our win. I loved football. I heard my mother yell, "Mona baby I hope you're ready! Your dad is waiting." I was spending the day with my father, the love of my life. Grabbing my all-white North Face coat with the matching hat and my white Polo gloves, I followed Daddy out to the truck.

"Daddy where are we going?" I jumped up and down excited. "Don't worry it's a surprise princess," he said. "I love you Daddy," I yelled. I opened the passenger side door to my father's all-white Cadillac truck with gold plated rims. I loved to ride shotgun when I was with my father because all the neighborhood bitches couldn't stand me and were a bunch of damn haters. My father was his own worst enemy; he stayed trying to outdo himself. Once I got in and fastened my seat belt and

Roni J.

Daddy did the same he looked at me and said, "Give me your eyes baby girl." Whenever Daddy told me that, it meant for me to look him straight in the eye, so I did. "No matter what, whenever you're talking to someone always look them dead in the eyes Monie. The eyes are the window to the soul, the only way you know someone is telling the truth. If they can't lock eyes, they're lying; always remember that. I love you princess," he said looking me straight in the eye. "Ok Daddy," was all I could say smiling with a big ass smile, showing all my pearly whites.

Thirty minutes later, we were in front of Towson Town Center, a huge mall out in the suburbs. Mainly rich people and white people shopped there. "Oh my God we're going shopping Daddy?" I was so pumped up I could barely get myself together. Shopping was what I lived for. "Yes princess, it's your birthday. You're turning the big 13; you're officially off the clock. It's time for you to pick out your own clothes," he said and smiled. "But my birthday is 3 days away Daddy," I said with a big smile as I thought to myself "I wish Mya were here."

"I'm so excited Daddy thank you so much!"

A Daughters Rage

"You're very welcome, now where do you want to go first?" he asked.

I didn't know where to start; I just knew I wanted everything. "Let's go to the Apple store Daddy, I want the new iPhone," I screamed. "Ok let's go," Daddy said smiling. He knew I was about to go crazy spending his money.

"I have to find a fly outfit for my birthday party this weekend too Daddy."

My daddy smiled at me as he said "Ok baby whatever you want."

Three hours later, I was tired, sleepy, and hungry. I had run through the mall like a maniac. I got all kinds of shit at my daddy's expense; he always spoiled me. Loving every minute of my happiness my daddy asked "Ok princess what do you want to eat?" It didn't take a lot to come up with my answer "I want pizza," I yelled. Shaking his head my dad said "Ok we can stop at Papa Johns on the way home." He laughed because he knew pizza was my favorite. We were walking through the parking lot with lots of bags; both our hands were full and I was ready to unload all my stuff into Daddy's truck. On our way to the truck, I saw this bitch from school named Tyra. Tyra and I

Roni J.

couldn't stand each other; that bitch was a hater. I just looked at her and smiled while mouthing the words, "Now run tell that bitch!" I could tell she read my lips because she frowned and rolled her eyes. Ole hating ass bird. I laughed climbing up in the truck while daddy loaded the bags.

On the way home, I fell asleep in the truck but I woke up when I overheard my daddy arguing on the phone with someone. "Look I don't have time for this shit, I'm tired of these arguments every other day, if you want to leave then go, but you're not taking my daughter," he yelled into the phone. The mention of me had my ears perked; he must've been talking to my mother. Lately they had been arguing every damn day, literally. When Daddy got off the phone, he was upset. Whenever he got angry there was a big ass vein that would pop up in the center of his forehead and it was bulging. I pretended to be asleep. He picked up the phone and called someone. "Hey how are you?" he asked. "Yeah I know she just called me ramping and raging. This shit has to stop. She's my wife and has a right to know. I will call you tomorrow." He hung up. Whoever he was talking to, he was talking to them about my mother.

I wondered who that was, and what my

A Daughters Rage

mother had a right to know. I suddenly wasn't hungry anymore. I stretched pretending as if I'd just woken up and I said, "I don't feel too good Daddy, my stomach hurts." I mumbled with a frown. "Ok you want to go straight home then?" he asked looking a little nervous. "Yes Daddy," I replied. Later that night I was in my room putting away the gifts Daddy bought me. I heard my parents yelling and arguing. "Here we go again," I thought. "Why are you keeping secrets from me Ray? I'm your fucking wife," my mother was yelling and crying. "I'm not going through this again Sandy! You can think what the fuck you want to think but I advise you to stop fucking yelling while my daughter is in the next room," Daddy said angry. "Your daughter? Are you fucking serious? If you were so worried about Mona then why the fuck are you fucking around on her mother with some dirt bag ass whore huh?" Mommy was still yelling. "Watch your fucking mouth Sandy; it's your last warning!" Daddy was heated with anger. I could hear it all in his voice. Then I heard a door slam. I ran to my bedroom door and opened it. Peeking my head out I saw my mother on her knees on the floor crying. Walking up to her I asked, "Mommy what's wrong, where's Daddy?" She looked up at me, her eyes were red as

Roni J.

fire and her response was, "Go to bed baby girl." Even though I didn't want to leave her there upset, I turned to walk away and went back to my room. I'd never seen my mother so upset. I went into my room, climbed on my bed, and cried for what seemed like hours. For some reason I felt like everything was about to change. I heard my mother talking on the phone but I couldn't understand what she was saying. All I heard was, "Yes, let's do it." I didn't know what that meant, but I could tell that it wasn't good because of how she said it. I laid there staring at the ceiling, squeezing my eyelids closed; trying to force myself to sleep so the night could just end. I wanted Daddy and Mommy to be happy again. I said my nightly prayer and off to sleep I went.

Early the next morning I awoke to my mother screaming and crying, "Noooooooooo!" My heart was beating fast; I jumped out of my bed, and took off running down the hall towards my parent's bedroom. I peeked in, it was empty, and then I heard voices and walkie-talkie radios coming from downstairs. It was the police. I slowly walked down the stairs; my feet felt like bricks with each step I took until I reached the bottom and I heard the officer say, "I'm sorry Mrs. Ramirez, but the

A Daughters Rage

gunshot victim has already been identified as your
husband Mr. Ray Ramirez."

I fainted.

Roni J.

A Daughters Rage

Two years later....

I was a bitch from the moment I slithered out of Sandy's old dirty diseased pussy. Everybody who had encountered me said I was a bitch and pure evil. Shit, what could I say? It was all true. I was born to cause havoc on the dirty streets of Baltimore.

It was 25 degrees but felt more like it was below zero outside because of the wind-chill and my mother had me standing outside the house while she sucked a dope boy named Kevin's dick. It wasn't as if I didn't know how her dirty ass got down. I could've just gone in my room and listened like I always did. "I hate that bitch," I mumbled. We didn't have a porch; we had three steps in front of our house, which were covered with a thin layer of ice due to it being so damn cold out. The frown on my face could have scared the devil himself. My feet and hands were beginning to get numb and I couldn't feel my damn face. "Hey there Mona," Mrs. Lucille our neighbor and my best friend's mom said to me. Mrs. Lu was so pretty and she always smelled so good. My mother hated her. She had the biggest ass I'd ever seen in my 14 yrs. The

Roni J.

boys in the hood called her "Big booty Lu."

"I want an ass like you when I get older Mrs. Lu."

She laughed and said, "You're going to have so much more Monie." She winked her eye before inviting me in. "Do you want to come in out the cold baby? I can fix you some hot chocolate," she offered. I was trying to understand what she meant by me having so much more. The way I saw it I'd be lucky to be alive on my birthday, which was coming up in a week. Before I could accept her offer, Kevin tapped me on my shoulder and got my attention. I looked up and he handed me a $20 bill while smiling. "What's this for?" I asked. "Get yourself something to eat lil mama," he said. All I could do was smile at his generosity. He was always so nice to me, but for some reason I always got an eerie feeling whenever he was around. Out of the corner of my eye, I noticed Sandy looking out of the curtain in the living room window. I walked in the house smiling because I was only going to add that twenty to my stash. My smile quickly turned to a frown. "POW!" Sandy slapped the piss out of me literally. I was somewhat used to her abuse by then; I just stood there pissing on myself. "I can't stand your lil ugly ass; you prance around

A Daughters Rage

here like you're the queen. I'm the only queen in this bitch so I suggest you get with the program or die like your selfish ass father," she yelled. I could never understand why the bitch hated me so much when I looked just like her. Whenever she would hit me, I refused to cry which only made her angrier. I just stood there staring at her. "Oh you a bad bitch huh?" she asked. "Now give me that $20 Kevin just gave you."

"What $20?" I asked. I would've given it to her if she would've asked instead of demanding. She needed it more than I did. "Raggedy bitch," I thought. She wrapped her right hand around my throat and squeezed. I looked at her with piercing, pleading eyes for her to let me go, but she just squeezed tighter. It felt like the life was leaving my body, so I dropped the twenty-dollar bill on the floor. When Sandy realized I dropped it, "Pow!" She hit me again. "That's for lying; conniving ass. Now go upstairs, wash your funky pissy ass, then when you're done come mop my damn floor," she yelled in my face, and some spit flew from her mouth falling on my lip. I almost flipped the fuck out. I started to slowly back away from her, fearing she'd hit me again and I'd snap. Once I reached the bottom of the stairs, I turned around and took off

Roni J.

running up the steps straight to the bathroom. I rushed in and slammed the door. From a distance, I heard Sandy yell, "Don't be slamming my doors bitch!"

Taking off my coat, I turned on the shower and stepped in the tub fully dressed. I just stood there while the water ran down on me. For the first time since my daddy died 2yrs ago, I cried. I cried so hard I threw up right there in the shower. I cried for my father who had been killed. Rumor was some stick-up boys ran up on him while he was parked in his truck and shot him once in the head. I didn't believe that shit. My father would never allow himself to be caught off guard like that, and to that day, I thought Sandy was behind it. "I miss you Daddy," I said softly. I cried for Sandy too because deep down I loved my mother, but that bitch had to go. On my own life, I promised I was going to kill her for my daddy and me. I remembered Sandy used to love me, but now the bitch treated me like shit. She didn't do shit but drink and fuck all day. She was broke as hell and got a once a month check that barely paid the bills. The abuse started about a month after my father died. I was his princess. I had straight A's in school and for that, my daddy had spoiled me. I didn't

A Daughters Rage

have many friends. The girls at my school hated me
and I had no clue why. My mother used to say it
was because I was half Puerto Rican and half Black.
I had long curly hair, my skin was the color of
caramel, and my eyelashes were naturally long. I
have one dimple in my left cheek and a beauty
mark on my right cheek. The only girl who would
talk to me was Mya Stewart who was my best
friend. We have been best friends since first grade. I
sometimes wished Mya was my sister. I loved her
so much. I smiled because Mya will be home this
week and it will be the first time I'd seen her since
she moved to her dad's a few months ago. I was so
excited. For a moment, I forget about my pathetic,
abusive ass life. Sandy had told me I was a woman
now and that I had to fend for myself. I was out
there sucking and fucking just to get a meal. That
couldn't be my life, or was it? My grandmother had
wanted me to go live with her in Miami when my
father died, but Sandy wouldn't allow it. She
wanted me to stay there with her so she could turn
my life into a living hell. Most nights I snuck out
and ended up staying the night with one of my
tricks. I didn't fuck with nothing but ballers and
businessmen who were only looking for a night of
good sex. Most of them were regulars I dealt with
on certain days of the week. I made a lot of money.

Roni J.

Sandy didn't know shit about it and my plan was to keep it that way. I was saving all my money so I could get the fuck away from the miserable ass bitch. I had about six thousand dollars stacked. A lawyer dude I was fucking kept telling me I could live in his penthouse, but fuck all that. I needed my own space and if I went that route, it would fuck up how I made my money. That nigga might want to keep me to himself and I couldn't allow that. Stepping out of the shower after peeling my wet clothes off, I wrapped myself in my towel and headed to my room.

A Daughters Rage

Sandy

I swear Kevin think I'm playing with his ass. He must not understand who the fuck I am. "I need a fucking drink," I thought while pouring some Absolut Vodka on a few cubes of ice and punching Kevin's number in my iPhone. "What up?" Kevin answered. "What the fuck did I tell you about being so friendly with Mona?" I asked fuming. "What the fuck are you talking about?" he asked. Before I could reply, he'd hung up. I couldn't believe that motherfucker hung up on me. "Ahhhhhhhh," I screamed throwing the phone and knocking over a beautiful Egyptian vase that Ray had given me for my birthday one year. I started to think about Ray. "Why Ray?" I asked out loud. "I loved you my whole life but the secrets I couldn't handle." I'd been thinking a lot about Ray lately. Ever since he died, I hadn't been the same. I remembered back when I met Ray in high school. Lake Clifton used to be one of the best schools in Baltimore in my time, but like everywhere else, it was infested with drug dealers, and Ray Ramirez was the head of it all. Ray was six feet tall with caramel skin that was as soft as butter. He was cut up like fresh Columbian coke and had the sexiest smile I'd ever seen. He had dimples that were so deep he didn't have to smile for you to see them. And to top it off, he had a head full of thick jet-black curls. Every time I saw Ray, I got moist.

One day I was walking up the stairs headed to math class, not paying attention. I walked right into Ray. "I'm so sorry I wasn't paying attention," I said. Ray grabbed my shoulders and said, "No problem beautiful," looking directly in my big brown eyes. Then he disappeared. That was the first time I was that close to Ray but it damn sure wouldn't be the last.

A Daughters Rage

Kevin

"Yo I'm telling you my nigga, that bitch Sandy is going to make me seriously hurt her Lo!" I was yelling and pacing the floor talking to my homie Lo. I met Lo two years earlier when my OG Gotti introduced us. I did a run with him and we'd been cool ever since. "What the fuck that hoe do now?" Lo asked. The expression on my face showed my concern "She's always threatening to hurt lil Mona. I don't know what it is about lil mama, but I feel drawn to her like I have to protect her from that bitch," I said. Scratching my head and turning to my friend with a serious expression I said "You know rumor is she had that nigga Ray set up, but I don't think her dumb ass is smart enough to set a plan like that in motion."

"Don't underestimate a hoe ever," Lo said laughing.

"Yeah you may be right because I met her through Vanessa's crazy ass. My momma told me Vanessa wasn't shit, but back when I was nickel and diming, Ness used to look out for me. She even helped me on a few licks. It's fucked up that she

Roni J.

tried killing herself and got put in that crazy house and shit, and don't nobody know why. I'm still confused about that shit."

Lo was shaking his head as he said "Shit my nigga, you're as blind as they come. Ness got a hold of some bad product and went crazy," Lo had a smirk on his face. The way he laughed made me feel uneasy. Then he said something that really threw me for a loop. "My nigga why the fuck you care about lil shorty so much? You want to fuck or something? You're always in your feelings about shorty, damn," Lo yelled with a fucked up look on his face. The air was becoming a little thick with tension "Yo, you better watch your fucking mouth, she's a child, fuck you mean," I said angrily thinking that nigga was sick minded. Lo didn't care how shit sounded he just kept talking "Yeah she may be a child but you and I both know how she gets down, and she got a fat ass too," he said. I just stared at that motherfucker as if he was crazy. "Yo you're a sick motherfucker! I think it's time for you to dip out my nigga!" Lo laughed and said, "Alright, you got that." Then he grabbed his gun, stopped, and looked at me before leaving. There was something unnerving about the way he looked at me. My heart was beating so fast it sounded like

A Daughters Rage

a drum in my chest. Still watching the door that Lo just walked out of I thought to myself "What the fuck just happened?" That nigga Lo was a sick motherfucker, looking at Mona like that. Something wasn't right about that nigga. I'd soon find out exactly what it is, but at the moment, the loud was calling me. I rolled my blunt and laid back across the sofa, propping my feet up on the table knowing damn well my momma didn't play that shit. I laughed and said to myself, "Momma not here though."

Roni J.

A Daughters Rage

Mona

After my shower, I went to lie down but I couldn't get comfortable. My wife beater was sticking to my skin and my panties felt glued to my ass because I was sweating so badly. Sandy's bitch ass had the heat on 100. What the fuck was wrong with her? As I lay there sweating and contemplating another shower I heard the secret tap from my best friend. Mya and I had been best friends since 1st grade but due to Mrs. Lu working so many hours at the hospital Mya lived at her dad's house. We came up with the secret tap to let her know I was ok. She knew about the abuse, and how badly Sandy treated me since my father died. I got up out of the bed and mashed my ear to the wall. I tapped four times and I heard Mya say, "I love you Monie." I smiled, and said, "I love you to Mya." I quickly got dressed, put my coat back on, and took off running downstairs so I could go be with my best friend. Sandy was sitting in the living room drinking as always. "Where the fuck you think you going?" she asked. "I was coming to ask you if I could go watch a movie with Mya," I replied. I wasn't going to ask her ass shit. I was going to just leave like I always did. "Yeah

Roni J.

whatever. See if Lu's uppity ass is going to feed you because I ain't cooking shit," she said with an attitude. She couldn't stand Mrs. Lu but didn't have a reason to feel that way. Sandy was just a miserable bitch. "Do you ever," I mumbled. "No I don't and I don't give a fuck if you eat or not! And the next time you get slick bitch I'm going to break your fucking neck," she yelled. I waved her off, left to go knock on Mrs. Lu's door, and out of the corner of my eye, I thought I saw that nigga Lo. Lo was a crazy nigga and everybody in the hood knew he wasn't right. They knew he was the one who set his house on fire killing his mother and brother but it could never be proven. I tried my best to stay out of the nigga's path but I couldn't help but to look at him. He was weird as shit. It had to be only twenty degrees out and that fool had on a thin black hoodie. He must have been on that shit again. I shook my head and looked away. Before I could knock on the door Mya swung the door open and wrapped her little chubby arms around my neck so tightly I couldn't breathe. I managed to say, "I missed you too!"

"Come on Monie my mom went to the market. We've got snacks and she's ordering pizza, we've got so much to talk about," Mya said excitedly. I was so happy to be with my best friend. I was waiting for the time to tell Mya my plan. We didn't keep secrets from one another. Mya was sweet and innocent. She didn't understand my pain. She had both her parents and even though they were divorced, they treated her like a princess still. Mrs. Lu was a nurse's aide and Mr. Stewart was a firefighter. Mya had everything. I used to have everything too until my daddy died. She was always sharing with me. We called each other sisters. I was an only child but Mya had a younger brother. I got comfy and prepared for my time with my best friend.

Roni J.

A Daughters Rage

Lorenzo "Lo"

I knew that lil bitch saw me. I couldn't wait to get a hold of her. I was going shove my dick down her throat since she liked sucking dick. I knew I was going to have to kill Kevin, the bitch ass nigga. He never knew his father so I wondered how he'd feel when he found out Ray was his father. Unknown to him I only let him in on the plan so niggas wouldn't put shit together and figure out that it was me who killed Ray's bitch ass. I had him under the impression that I was going to pick up some money and that shit might get ugly so I needed him to drive the car. Green ass nigga didn't even know he was involved in his own father's murder. Before I killed my mother that bitch finally told me who my father was. All those motherfuckers were always quick to say I was crazy, but they didn't understand what happened to me as a child. It was only right that I killed my mother and lil brother. He was only a baby; he never knew life so he didn't miss out on shit. God didn't and don't give a fuck about me but maybe he understood that I killed my brother for his own safety. I couldn't allow him to live in a world that was so dangerous. My phone vibrated in my pocket. I dug in my pocket grabbing it, and pressing the answer button I yelled, "Hello?"

"Where the fuck you been?" the unknown caller asked.

"I've been around," I said while laughing.

"Why the fuck are Kevin and Sandy still breathing? They're the only ones who can connect you to the murder," the caller said.

"Kevin ain't no snitch. Believe me when I say that. Besides his ass was a part of it and he don't even know it. Now Sandy ass is scared Mona's going to find out she had her father killed."

"I don't give a fuck about either of them, but Mona is another story. Bring her to me!" Click. They hung up. "Fuck! Fuck! Fuck," I yelled. Now I had to put a plan in motion. I walked down the alley headed to my bitch Tonya's house. I hoped she had cooked because I was hungry as shit and I hoped she was ready to get that ass busted open. I laughed. I'd rather fuck ass than pussy; that was another thing that set me apart from the rest of those niggas. Pussy wasn't good to me; I mean I fucked it every so often, but I wasn't not a fan of it.

A Daughters Rage

Mona

I was still chilling out with my Mya having a good time catching up on everything when she said "So Monie, what's the plan for your birthday? I told my mom we wanted to go skating." I felt a tightness in my chest "I'm not sure what I want to do, my birthday two years ago is all I keep thinking about, and it was the last time I spent with him," I said sadly looking down at the floor. The tightness in my chest felt as though it was getting worse "I miss my Daddy!" I started to cry. "I know Monie I'm sorry," Mya said hugging me. "It's not your fault Mya. I just knew I would have had a big party with lots of gifts if my dad was alive. I was his princess." The more I thought about my daddy the more I felt my mother had something to do with his death. I remember them arguing about secrets or some shit like that, and the next day my daddy was dead. On my life, I was going to get to the bottom of that shit. For Sandy's sake, she better hope and pray she wasn't behind it because what I planned to do to her if she was would have her wishing she died with my father.

Wiping away the tears from my cheeks I

Roni J.

said "Ok Mya tell Mrs. Lu skating sounds like fun."
"Yay!" She hugged me. "Oh my Monie we're going
to have so much fun. I promise." Mya was Jumping
up and smiling; she ran off to tell Mrs. Lu that we
were going skating.

Even though my birthday was a whole
week away, Mrs. Lu decided to take us that day
because she would be working on my actual
birthday. So later that day Mrs. Lu took Mya and I
skating at Shake and Bake skating rink. She bought
me a big chocolate cake and we had hotdogs and
soda. We skated so long we tired ourselves out.
While Mrs. Lu and Mya went to the bathroom, I sat
on the bench to catch my breath and take my skates
off. I felt someone touch the back of my neck, and
when I turned to see who it was I almost threw up
everything that I ate. It was crazy ass Lo! He looked
deranged. "Sick fucker," I thought. "Now look you
lil bitch you can walk out of here with me like we're
together, or you can scream and make a scene.
Either way you're going with me so make a choice,"
he said whispering. I froze. I didn't know what to
do. "Why the fuck is Lo trying to take me with
him?" I thought. I was looking at Lo like he had
lost his damn mind "He's going have to kill my ass
because I'm not leaving with his crazy ass!" I

started to scream until I saw the gun sticking out of the front of his pants. He didn't even give me a chance to put my shoes and coat on. He grabbed my wrist so hard it felt like it was going to break. I was scared so I just walked out with him. As we were leaving, I heard Mya calling my name but I kept walking.

He had a gray pickup truck double-parked in the street. He walked me around to the passenger's side, opened the door, threw my ass in the truck, and said, "One move and I won't hesitate to shoot your ass, now try me." I was too scared to look at his ass let alone do something dumb. He was not the type of nigga that you wanted to test. He jumped in the truck and sped off as if we had just robbed a bank. We flew down the block, through alleys, and bending corners. That nigga was really in a hurry and that was what got me worried. Pulling onto MLK, we stopped in front of a shabby looking house. It looked familiar. "I think I've been here before," I thought as he said through gritted teeth "Get the fuck out and you better not fuck with me bitch." We walked up the porch steps hand in hand as if we were a fucking couple. "What the fuck is this nut ass nigga about to do to me?" I wondered. Once inside he took my ass

Roni J.

down to the basement.   "Something smells dead down in this bitch," I thought as I looked around for the cause of the smell. Then out of nowhere, he punched the shit out of me on the side of my head and everything went dark.

A Daughters Rage

Sandy

"What the fuck you mean Mona left with Lo?" I was yelling so loud I was giving myself a damn headache. "Mya and I went into the bathroom while Mona sat on the bench right outside the bathroom," Lu tried to explain. "I don't give a fuck what you say! You left my child alone," I was still yelling not understanding.

"Now you may be upset Sandy for your own reasons, but let's be real. You don't give a fuck about that lil girl. Ever since Ray died, you've treated her as if it's her fault. I may be wrong but to me it seems like you feel guilty about something," Lu said with a smirk on her ashy ass face. "Bitch please! You don't know shit about me! And if you ever say that shit again I'll fuck your uppity ass up," I threatened.

"If you say so bitch, I've given the police all the info they need so I pray they find Mona safely. Mya and I have been all up and through this neighborhood looking for her but there's no sign of her. Please, if you don't mind, can you keep me posted," Lu said as she was walking to the door to leave.

"Bitch I ain't telling you shit! Get the fuck out of my house." They left and I slammed my door, but as soon as I did, the police knocked. I started not to open that shit but I did and swung that motherfucker open with an attitude. "Hello Ma'am, I'm Officer Jake Robinson, and this is my partner Romello Johnson. Are you Sandy Ramirez?" the officer asked.

"Yes Officer I am, may I help you?"

I remembered those motherfuckers, they were the same two who knocked on my door and told me my husband was dead. That was two years ago but I never forget a face. "Yes we got word that your daughter Mona Ramirez was abducted by a Lorenzo Baxter. Is that true?" he asked. "I don't know for sure Officer but Mona is hot in her ass. She may have left with him voluntarily," I snapped.

"Your daughter is 14 years old correct?"

"This mother fucker is fine but appears to be a lil off," I thought. "Yes and what does that mean?" I asked. "Ma'am your 14yr old daughter was possibly abducted and you're blaming her?" he asked with a raised eyebrow. "Look, are you done?

A Daughters Rage

I got shit to do," I responded with an attitude. That shit with Mona's lil grown ass was pissing me the fuck off. "Here's my card. If you hear or see anything call me," Officer Robinson said handing me his card. "Yeah ok, will do." I slammed the door.

"Is it me or does she seem to not give a fuck that her child has been taken by a known criminal?" Jake asked. "Yeah something is seriously wrong with that bitch," Romello responded. "We'll tell the captain to put a car on the house. I got a feeling she's hiding something." They both walked back to the squad car and pulled off.

Roni J.

A Daughters Rage

Kevin

"What the fuck?" I'm trying to get my thoughts together. "Did I hear you correctly?" I was pacing again as I seemed to do every time I get upset or nervous about something. "Did you say Lo's got Mona? When? Where? How? What the fuck is going on," I yelled in the phone. "Yeah she went to Shake and Bake with Lu and Mya. Lu said she was on the bench outside the bathroom waiting for them to come out and as they were coming out Mya saw Mona leaving with Lo. He had his arm around her waist or some shit like that," Sandy said. I was fucking heated! That motherfucker had gone too far. "Look Sandy hold tight. I'm going to look for Lo and find out what the fuck is going on, we both know Mona didn't willingly go with his crazy ass."

"Yeah ok whatever," she said hanging up the phone. I knew something was wrong with the nigga but why the fuck would he take Mona. What was his plan? I swore on everything that nigga better not lay a finger on her or I'd kill his ass! Grabbing my keys and almost tripping over the end table I left my house, hopped in my car, and

Roni J.

drove down Pennsylvania Ave asking niggas on the block if they had seen Lo. Everybody acted all scared and shit. I spotted a crack head named Jerry. "Let me ask him," I thought. Jerry knew everything about the shit that went down in the hood. "Aye yo Jerry, come here for a sec big homie," I yelled out to him. He started to limp his dirty ass over to my car. "He- he- he- hey Kevin," he stuttered. "Yo have you seen Lo?"

"Ye- ye –yeah and he had Ray's daughter with him," he said and I got a glimpse of that fool's mouth. There was one big tooth hanging down that was discolored and it looked like there was shit on his teeth. It was annoying the fuck out of me. I shook my head. "Did you see which way they went," I asked. "N-n-n-n no." He looked like he was lying. "Look Jerry this shit is serious. I need to find him right the fuck now," I said a little aggressively hoping to scare him so I wouldn't have to beat his ass.

"I-I- I -don't know," he said looking away. I was so fucking pissed I pulled off rolling over the nigga's feet. I heard him scream and yell out but I didn't give a fuck! I had to find them before he hurt her.

A Daughters Rage

Lorenzo

"Yo I got the package," I said yelling into my phone. "Where the fuck you at?" Santana asked. "I'm on MLK at Ness's old house. In the basement."

"Did anybody see you go in there?" he asked. The nigga seemed really paranoid asking me all those fucking questions. "Man I know what the fuck I'm doing, didn't nobody see me," I replied, heated. "I know you better watch your fucking tongue nigga," Santana responded. "Man fuck you! Hurry up and come get this lil bitch before my dick goes in her mouth," I said laughing. "You're a sick motherfucker but I don't care what you do. All I'm trying to do is find the money that Ray owes me and if I don't, you're going to have a problem. You're the one who told me she knew where it was," Santana said still making threats.

"Those motherfuckers don't know who I am but they soon will," I thought. "Nigga just hurry the fuck up," I told him. I hung up. Mona was sitting on an old milk crate in the center of the floor. To her right there was an old mattress standing up against the wall and a dead rat was to the left caught in a trap. The smell was unbearable. The basement was dimly lit but she could see me clearly. For the first time I noticed how pretty she was. She was a little out of it from the punch I gave her in the head. I walked up to her standing right in front of her so when she lifted her head it would be in my crotch. "So Mona, word on the street is you like sucking dick. I'm going to take the tape off your mouth and if you scream, I'm going to break your fucking neck. You understand?" I asked her before removing the tape. She nodded her head. "Ok good. Open your mouth," I yelled. "No Lo I'm not sucking your dick," she said with an attitude that only pissed me off more. "Say what," I yelled grabbing her by the back of her neck. "You're not going to do what?" Before she could say it again, I grabbed her by her hair tightly and snapped her neck back. I thought I broke that shit. Shit, I had heard a cracking sound. "Ok, ok I'll do it," she said crying. She looked me in my eyes with a look of pure hate, but she didn't seem scared at all. "If you know like I know that's your best choice," I said.

A Daughters Rage

Mona

My hands were tied behind my back and my neck was hurting so bad. I thought maybe I could bite that motherfucker, but then I remembered someone else was on the way and he'd probably kill my ass. As he unzipped his pants, I smelled a strong fishy smell. "What the fuck is that smell?" I asked. "Shut the fuck up bitch and suck this big motherfucker," Lo yelled still holding my neck. I started to suck his dick but the smell was so bad I felt like I was about to throw up. My nostrils were burning so bad and his dick seemed like it was growing by the fucking second. I felt his dick touching the back of my throat and he was literally pumping my face like it was a pussy. I closed my eyes and I cried. "H-m-mmm! G-r-rrrr!" He was grunting which could only mean he was about to cum. "Arg-hhhh-hhhh," he moaned and let off in my mouth. My mouth was filled with his cum and I was literally choking. His cum tasted like poison and I couldn't hold it back. I threw up all over his dick, shoes and pants. "E-www you nasty little bitch you threw up on my shit," he yelled. He was fuming, he was about to fuck me up! Then we both turned the same direction. We heard a set of voices

45

Roni J.

outside. I was in thinking mode then. "Was that Kevin's voice I heard? Is he in on this? What the fuck is going on," I thought. "I'm about to go outside and see what the fuck is going on, if you budge I'll blow your fucking brains out," Lo said before walking up the basement steps leaving me alone. The taste of his cum and the smell of the dead rat in the corner had me literally sick to my fucking stomach so I threw up again. That time all over myself.

A Daughters Rage

Kevin

As I was riding down MLK, I saw who appeared to be Santana but my eyes had to be playing tricks on me. Last I heard that nigga was in the pen. I thought he was alone until I saw Lo. My mind was racing. I thought that nigga was in upstate New York serving a life sentence, so why was he here? So many thoughts were running through my mind. Why was he here? Ness hadn't been around there in over a year and even if she was what was the connection? When I saw Lo appear from nowhere, he was sweating. He looked nervous and he was yelling. I got out of my car and began to walk towards them on the porch. "Aye Lo what's up," I yelled out. I could tell Santana was saying something to him but I couldn't hear what. Santana went in the house and Lo walked towards me. "Ain't shit up lil nigga. You don't belong around these parts, so get the fuck from around here before your face ends up on a milk carton my nigga," he said while tapping his gun that was visible on his waist. I noticed some shit on his pants that looked like throw up. That nigga had done a complete turnaround. He was acting real shady when I was with his ass earlier in the day. "What the fuck you watching my dick for nigga?" he asked. "Nigga I ain't watching your dick, but it looks like you threw up on yourself G," I responded. "Don't worry about my dick nigga just get the fuck on about your business," Lo said with an attitude. "You real hostile Lo but it's all good G, you got that. I just wanted to know if you saw Mona's lil ass around because Sandy called me and said she hasn't seen her," I said. He looked nervous but then his face changed to a smirk and he said, "Naw I haven't seen her lil hoe ass, you might want to try looking down on the block." Then he busted out laughing. I turned to walk off; his behavior was off more than usual. It seemed as if had he just turned into a totally different person right in front of me, but if that nigga thought I was just going to go on about my business because he told me to, he was sadly mistaken.

A Daughters Rage

In the Basement: Mona

"Where's the money?" Santana asked.

"I don't know about no money, I swear my daddy never talked about his business when I was around," I said. I looked him straight in the eyes when I said it; Daddy told me the eyes speak the truth every time. "Sandy knows," I blurted out. Truth was I didn't know if she did or not, I just knew I didn't.

"She's fucking lying," Lo shouted.

"Look little girl your daddy owes me big time and I want what's rightfully mine, now I'm going to ask you again, do you know where the money is?" Santana resembled my father so much it was creepy. He looked really calm though. He looked me dead in my eyes and it sent chills down my spine.

"No I don't know," I said still staring at him. "Gag her Lo, she's telling the truth. Let's just hope Sandy doesn't play games with me because I'll have to kill her silly ass," Santana said. "Hold the fuck up, how you know she's telling the truth?" Lo

Roni J.

asked.

"Don't worry about that. Just gag her and let's get the fuck out of here," Santana said as he walked up the basement steps. I could tell he didn't want to hurt me.

"I will be back bitch," Lo said looking at me with fire in his eyes. Santana looked like my dad. Daddy told me he had a brother but that he was locked up for life. I didn't think it could be him, but I couldn't shake what I was feeling. There was also the fact that he looked me in the eyes and knew I was telling the truth. Could that be my uncle? I was confused; shit was getting crazier by the minute. The smell of that dead rat in the corner was getting the best of me and I felt like I was about to throw up again. I knew one thing for sure; if I made it out of that shit, those bitches were going learn that I was not to be fucked with. I was my father's daughter and nobody knew or understood the connection I had with him, or what he taught me.

A Daughters Rage

Kevin

I realized my car was still parked out front so I ran across the lawn, hopped in my car, and pulled into the alley behind two big dirty ass dumpsters, hoping they didn't spot me. I got out and peeked around the corner. I saw Santana and Lo pull off in a black Ford F150 pick-up truck.

Making sure no one saw me, I ran back across the lawn. Seeing a brick in the grass, I used it to break the basement window. Once I got all the glass out, I crawled through the window and jumped down to the floor. I spotted Mona tied up with duct tape on her mouth. Her eyes were bulging and she was scared. "Hey lil mama. I'm not here to hurt you, we've got to get you out of here," I explained. She was nodding her head. "First, I have to untie your hands; you take the tape off while I untie your ankles. Mona, listen to me, we have to get to your mother before Lo and Santana."

"What is going on Kevin?" she asked. "I don't know Mona. It's all happening so fast," Mona still looked scared as she said "Santana looked like he could be my daddy's twin; could he be my uncle

Roni J.

Kevin?"

"I don't know what you're talking about Mona, but later for that. We have to get to Sandy and now." I grabbed her hand and we both ran up the steps and out the front door to my car. I sped off so fast I left tire marks in the street.

A Daughters Rage

Sandy

All of this shit was my fault! If I could've just understood and accepted that Ray was a man whore, he would've still been there with me. I remember the day my life took a turn for the worse. My childhood best friend Vanessa told me she saw Ray creeping out of Linda's house. I knew Linda wanted Ray from day one but he was mine. One day I decided to go over to confront the bitch and she gladly allowed me in her home. She started to talk before I got a chance to question her.

"Look Sandy, I already know why you're here. Truth is, me and Ray have been fucking off and on, but Ray had also made it clear that you're wifey and honestly I don't have a problem with it at all," she said and laughed.

I was about to choke that bitch when her son Lo walked in the room scowling at me. I couldn't stop staring at him. He looked so much like Ray and he even had the curly hair and dimples. I was about to ask if he was Ray's son but for some reason her eyes were begging me not to say a word and I didn't. As soon as Lo left out of the house, she blurted out, "Yes he's his son. I'm sorry you had to find out this way, but Lo doesn't know and Ray asked me not to speak of it to anyone." I felt like the wind left my lungs. I couldn't speak, shit I couldn't even move. "Sandy I'm sorry. Are you ok?" Linda asked. Before I knew it, I lost it. I grabbed that bitch by the throat and tried to squeeze the life out of her, but the front door swung opened and it was Lo. He jumped on me like a pit bull, punching and choking me. I let her go but he wouldn't let up until she told him to. "Lo it's ok baby stop," she yelled. He let me go and took off running through the house breaking shit; I used that distraction as my chance to get the fuck up out of there.

As I sat there thinking back to that day, I was crying uncontrollably, shaking, the room was spinning. That must have been guilt for my role in Ray's murder. When Vanessa told me about some stick up boy's she knew up in DC I put her on it. The plan was for them to rob Ray, take his precious money, and shake him up a bit. Not kill him. "Boo-ommm!" I heard a giant crash and I jumped. What the fuck was that? Then I heard voices. "Where that bitch at?"

"Oh my God, is that Lo in my fucking

house, and who's with him," I thought. I was standing in the middle of the floor, frozen and scared shitless. Next thing I knew I heard them running up my stairs. "Think Sandy think!" Before I could move, they both came rushing in my bedroom. "If you even think about screaming, I'll put a bullet in your fucking skull, you snake ass bitch," Lo screamed. I couldn't see the other guy because my back was turned. Then he spoke. "I'm here for one reason and one reason alone. And that is to collect my money." It was Santana, Ray's brother, I realized as I turned around. "What money?" I asked. "Pow!" He smacked me so hard I felt my tooth disconnect from my gum and my mouth immediately filled with blood. "Don't make me ask you again bitch," Santana said angrily. The pain from my tooth had me in shock and my vision was blurred. The salty taste in my mouth from my own blood had me feeling nauseated and I wasn't about to swallow that shit. I spit it out on the floor along with my tooth. My first thought was when and how was Santana released? "I don't know what money you're talking about Santana," I told him yelling.

"Bitch don't play with me, you know what money I'm talking about! I knew my brother and your grimy ass was his everything. He told you about my million and I want it or you'll be fucking joining him," he yelled in my face. "I swear to you Santana, I don't know what you're talking about. Ray didn't tell me shit about no money and especially not about any belonging to you." Ray had been gone for two years and that nigga showed up then asking about some money that wasn't even his.

"I'm sick of both of those bitches! First Mona said she didn't know and you believed her, but she also said Sandy knew. So who the fuck lying," Lo yelled. I was wondering, what the fuck he meant by Mona said I knew about the money. Maybe she knew something that I didn't. Ray and Mona were very close and there wasn't anything he wouldn't have done for his little princess. Maybe he told her about the money Santana was speaking about. "Hold up, when did Mona tell you this and where is my daughter Lo," I yelled. "Bitch we're the ones asking the questions. Now let's go," Lo said. He grabbed me by my neck forcing me to walk with him and Santana down the steps and out the door. I couldn't believe those niggas were kidnapping me in broad daylight like that shit was ok. I didn't fuck with nobody around there so didn't nobody give a

A Daughters Rage

fuck and they wouldn't report that shit to the police. I had to laugh; the irony. The next thing I knew I was in the trunk of a car.

Roni J.

A Daughters Rage

Mona

I'd never been scared of anything in my life because my father had told me not fear anything, but right at that moment, he was probably disappointed in me because I was scared as shit. I had no clue what the fuck was going on or what money Daddy owed Santana. If he was on his way to my house, nine times out of ten, he was going to hurt Sandy and that would take all the enjoyment from me. I wanted to be the one to make that bitch suffer. Maybe my grandma Selma knew but I was not trying to put her in any danger so I'd leave that alone for the moment. I was so deep in my thoughts I didn't hear shit Kevin was saying to me. "Mona, are you ok lil mama?" he asked. I said, "Huh?"

"Are you ok? You don't look too good and you're shaking," he asked looking from me then back towards the cars in front of him on the road. I didn't even realize my hands were shaking like leaves on a tree. "I'm-I-I'm ok I think." For the first time I caught a clear view of Kevin, even though it was a side view because he was driving. I thought I was cracking the fuck up from all the smacks upside my head thanks to Sandy, but Kevin resembled my dad in his younger days.

First Santana and then Kevin. Hell no, I just really missed my father. Shit even Lo looked like my dad so I knew I was tripping. I was going crazy in my thoughts. I didn't even notice were pulling up to my house. "Hold tight Monie. I'm going in, do not move," Kevin said.

"Why? I want to know if Sandy is ok," I said. Truth was I didn't give a fuck; I just wanted to be nosey and find out about the money. Mostly I needed my damn coat. It was freezing out that bitch. I wasn't worried about them finding my shit because I had a lock box my daddy gave me to keep my money and jewelry safe. Nobody would ever know where to look for my shit. I was good at hiding shit.

"It's not safe Monie. Santana and Lo are both dangerous and they don't know that I have you so please stay in here and duck low," he said before getting out of the car. I frowned. "Ok," I said. Little did he know I was not staying in the fucking car. I was getting the fuck out of there.

The front door was open a little bit. I couldn't see inside but as soon as Kevin walked in the house, I got out of there. I took off running barefoot cutting through the vacant houses and hit Rutland to North Ave. I ran straight up North Ave. I didn't know where the fuck I was going but what I did know was that I wasn't staying there and waiting for shit to get ugly. That was the dumbest shit ever; I had no coat or shoes. "What the fuck am I doing?" I asked myself. I got a quick thought as I remembered Daddy telling me if I was ever in trouble to go to Heads and he would help me. Heads was a young dude that my dad kept close to him. He was like a son and he showed him the ends and outs to the drug game. I thought he was about 18. Shit, I couldn't remember where he lived, but I knew it was not far from where I was. I had to find him, but first I had to get a coat, some shoes, and my damn iPhone. I missed my damn iPhone. Sandy took that too. I swore I hated that bitch! I needed to talk to Mya. I had to pee so bad so I went in McDonalds to use the bathroom. As I was walking in, I spotted an old lady sitting at a table eating some fries, right across from the bathroom. Damn I was starving all of a sudden. She saw me staring and immediately noticed something was wrong. "Excuse me; I'm not from around here. I kind of got lost with some friends; do you have a phone I can use to call my mom please?" Now why in the fuck would I tell that lady I got lost with some friends and I was standing in her damn face bare foot? I hoped that she wouldn't look down at my damn feet. The old lady had a warm smile and head full of grey hair with her glasses sitting on the tip of her nose. She looked up at me smiling with a french fry in her hand. She finally spoke after staring at me for a few minutes. Then the smile was gone. She looked worried. "You're a very beautiful young lady sweetheart, and I hope I'm not prying but where are your coat and shoes sweetie?" she asked. "Are you going to be ok? Do you need a ride some place?" She smiled.

"Thank you so much and yes Ma'am, I'll be fine. I just need to call my mom and thank you again."

"You're welcome young lady." She gave me the phone and I walked off to the side to use it. I was going to call Mya. I hoped and prayed she answered the phone. I was shaking because I was nervous and cold. It was a long shot; Mya usually didn't answer numbers she didn't recognize.

I was so nervous I felt like I was about to piss on myself. I was hungry and thirsty all at the same damn time. Oh my God, she was not answering. I should hang up. Just as I was about to hang up she answered. "Hello?"

"Mya it's me," I said.

"Oh my God Monie where are you? Are you ok? Did Lo hurt you?" She was yelling in my ear throwing me with all those questions. "I'm ok Mya. I need you to calm down there's a lot I need to tell you, but right now is not the time. I need you to do me a favor. I need my coat and some tennis shoes. I'm at the McDonalds on Broadway, using this old lady's cell phone. I need your help!" I was whispering so no one could hear my conversation.

"Sure ok what you need me to do? You know I'll do anything for you Monie," she said while crying.

"Please Mya don't cry!"

"I'm scared Monie." She was crying and it was pissing me off. "I know, me too, but you have to pull it together ok?" I told her. "Ok," she said. "Do you remember that dude named Heads who used to be with daddy all the time?" I asked. "Um I-I think so, you talking about the one with the bald head and tattoos?" she asked. "Yes that's him"

"What about him Monie? I mean he's crazy

as hell, his cousin Tammy lives next door to my dad and she said he be snapping and shit. Something about having some type of disorder."

"I don't care about that shit Mya, I have to find him. Daddy told me if I was ever in any trouble to go to him and he'd help me. Is there a way you can find out from his cousin where he lives for me?" I asked looking over at the old lady who was staring at me trying to figure out what I was talking about.

"I don't trust him Monie, but ok I can do that," she said in a low tone. "Ok I have to go, get in contact with her and I'll call you back as soon as I can."

"You know that I will Mona. I love you and please be careful," she said sounding as if she was about to break down again. "I know and I love you too Mya." I hung up. I walked over to the lady and she asked, "Is everything ok honey?"

"Yes Ma'am, but if you don't mind can you take me to my friend's house to get my coat and shoes?" I asked. She looked as if she knew I was lying about something but I didn't give a fuck. She allowed me to do what I needed to do so I said, "Thank you." I had to get back in my house some kind of way.

"Sure sweetie I'll take you. Just let me get my things," she said. She got up, walked over to the trashcan, and threw away almost a whole meal. My damn stomach was screaming and I was starving. "Ok baby where does your friend live?" the old lady asked as we were walking out the door to her car.

Roni J.

A Daughters Rage

Kevin

As soon as I walked up to the house I noticed the door was open which only meant those two crazy motherfuckers had already been there. The house was a mess and Sandy was gone. "What the fuck is going on?" I wondered out loud. I knew I had to get the fuck out of there before I started to look suspicious. I could see from the steps that Monie wasn't in the car. I told her ass not to move, that little girl was going to fuck around and get us both killed. Where the fuck was she? I massaged my temples because the whole situation was giving me a fucking headache. I didn't know why I felt that deep feeling of obligation to her. It was almost as if I was supposed to help and protect her. Maybe she went next door. I walked out and over to knock on the door. There was no answer so I knocked again. "Who is it?" a soft voice asked from the other side. The person sounded like they were crying and her voice was trembling. "My name is Kevin, I'm looking for Monie." I heard what sounded like locks being undone and the door opened. It was Mrs. Lu's daughter Mya. "Hey Mya, have you seen Monie?" I asked. She looked very worried, so I thought she knew something. "How do I know I can trust you won't hurt her?" she asked.

"Is she here?"

"Answer me first." She looked at me as if I was the enemy. "I'm not the bad guy I'm trying to help Monie," I told her. She was a little hesitant but then she said, "She called me about 15 minutes ago from McDonald's up on Broadway. She is supposed to be calling me back. She asked me to get her coat and shoes from her house."

"Damn so I need to go back in there and grab her shit. Ok Mya thanks. I'm going to go back in there and see if I can find her stuff," I told her.

"Ok," she said, "and please have her call me back."

"Aight I got you," I told her and she shut the door. I was leery as shit going back in the house but I couldn't have her outside in the cold like that. Spotting her pink and white North Face coat on the sofa, I grabbed it then ran up the steps to her room. The damn door was locked. "Shit," I yelled. I was going have to take her to get some damn shoes. I ran back out the door but that time I locked it. I didn't need the crack heads seeing the house open. They'd for sure see a come up! I hopped in my car and pulled off. I hoped she was still up at McDonald's. I was flying up North Ave. about to turn into McDonald's parking lot when I spotted Monie about to get in a car with an old lady. At the same time, she saw me. "Kevin," she yelled. I stopped the car right behind the old lady's car. She turned to the old lady, said something, then the lady hugged her and waved good-bye.

Monie walked up to my car, pulled the door open, and looking a little nervous she said, "Kevin I just don't feel I can trust anybody."

"I think I understand, but you have to trust me. I'm not going to let nothing happen to you Monie I promise."

"I don't know Kevin. Right now I don't trust nobody," she said looking away. "I feel you; we've got to get you somewhere safe," I responded.

"My dad told me if I ever got into trouble that I could go to this young dude named Heads who used to work for him. I have to find him," she said getting a little too excited. "Not to be disrespectful Monie, but your dad is gone and you're here. You don't know shit about that dude," I said shaking my head. "I know my dad wouldn't lie to me so I'm going to find him with or without

69

your help. I have to call Mya back because she is supposed to be getting the address for me," she said with an attitude. "Well since you think you're grown and don't need my help, here's my phone, call Mya."

A Daughters Rage

Mona

As I was sitting in the car with Kevin something felt off. I felt like I hurt his feelings so I apologized. "I'm sorry Kevin, I know deep down you're only trying to help, but ever since my dad died I feel like all I have is Mya and Mrs. Lu. Sandy doesn't seem to give a fuck about me, all she does is abuse me and leave me to fend for myself." My eyes started to water. "My own mother turned her back on me like I'm the enemy. I don't deserve this shit. I'm 14 years old and I'm out here sucking dick and fucking grown ass men who don't mind fucking children for a couple dollars just to eat. My daddy is probably turned over in his grave ashamed of me." I looked at Kevin and he was staring at me without blinking. The same feeling I got when Santana looked me in my eyes was the feeling I was getting then. Something didn't feel right. That shit was really weird.

"Sometimes in life Monie you have to do things you don't want to do, but have to for survival. I want you to promise me you will stop that shit. I will take care of you if I have to, but please stop fucking your body up with these grown ass men," he said looking at me with pleading eyes.

Roni J.

My God those eyes, there was something strange within them. It was as if I saw my daddy. He looked away.

"Ok I will stop," I said not believing my own statement. He looked back over at me and said, "I found out about a year ago that Carolyn Jones is my adoptive mother, I know who my birth mother is, but I never got the chance to meet my father. For all I know he could be one of these crack heads I serve every day," Kevin said. I could see the sadness in his eyes. "Wow Kevin I'm sorry to hear that," I said touching his leg. "It's ok I'm good, but I couldn't help but wonder why my birth mother gave me up and never told my dad I even existed. I have to keep pushing though because with or without either of them, my life goes on you know," he said looking at the road ahead. "Yeah I know," I said while looking at the phone in my hand, hoping and praying Mya was able to find out where Heads lived. I began dialing her number then Kevin grabbed my left hand, held it, and said, "Go ahead I'm right here with you." I smiled and dialed. She answered on the first ring.

"Hello," Mya answered. "Hey ma it's me." She was breathing hard in the phone as if she was running or something. "Monie oh my God Kevin

72

came here looking for you! Why is he involved in this too? Against my better judgment I told him to get your coat and shoes," she said out of breath. "No it's ok. I'm with Kevin right now. He's going to help me find Heads. Did you get the address for me?"

"Yes I have it but Tammy said he be on the block around this time and that he goes in every night around 10," Mya said sounding relieved. "Ok its only 6:30 now. Are you ok though Ma?" I asked.

"I'm ok if you're ok. My mom went to the store, but she asked if you were ok. She said that if you needed us we would be here for you," she said.

"You told her you talked to me?" I asked with a slight attitude.

"No, I didn't have to. She knows how close we are and that you would contact me first chance you got," she said and I smiled.

"Mrs. Lu really does know me huh? I'm calling you from Kevin's phone but I'll call you back and let you know what's going on," I told her. Then I almost forgot why the fuck I had called in the first place, the damn address. "What's the address ma?" I asked. "It's 2131 Chase Street," she

Roni J.

said. "Ok ma thanks. Love you," I said. "Ok I love you too," she said before hanging up. I looked at Kevin, "So what do we do now?"

"First we get you somewhere safe and then we have to find out where Lo and Santana took Sandy," he said looking a little confused. "Are we going to your house?" I asked.

"No my house isn't safe. That's the first place they'll look once they realize you're gone. There's a little hole in the wall motel spot down on North and Howard. It's not the best, but it's a spot you can go to for the night." He looked undecided.

"Me? You're not coming with me?" I asked looking at him as if he was crazy.

"I will get you the room and make sure you're ok, but I have to find your mother and I know by now Santana and Lo are looking for us both," he said.

"But I don't want to stay alone. I'm scared," I yelled.

"I'll be back as soon as I'm done, what do you want to eat?"

"Ok. I want some wings, fries, and a Pepsi,"

74

A Daughters Rage

I responded.

"Ok I'll go get that for you after we get you situated."

We pulled up to an old raggedy ass building. The shit looked vacant it was so run down. Kevin looked at me and said, "Let me go check you in. I'll be right back." That was some straight bullshit and I was in no position to complain but got damn that shit was a fucking dump! "Ok lil mama let's get you in," Kevin said getting back in the car. He pulled the car around to where the room was. We both got out of the car looking around making sure nobody saw us. After Kevin opened the door, I just stood there for a minute.

Looking around the room the place was a bigger fucking dump inside. There were cigarette burns in the carpet, the curtains were shabby and raggedy, and the paint on the walls was peeling. There was a wooden chair in the corner that looked like the moment I touched it the shit was going to fall apart. I didn't think I wanted to even lie down on the bed, but I was so tired I could barely keep my eyes open. It was almost 7pm and I'd had more shit happen to me in one day than most people had

Roni J.

in a lifetime. "I'll be right back," Kevin said before leaving. Lying down on the bed wrapped up in my coat and using my arm as a pillow, I balled up in the fetal position and closed my eyes.

A Daughters Rage

Sandy

Those motherfuckers had me tied up, and blindfolded in the trunk of Santana's car. I had pissed on my damn self and my face felt numb. I was so thirsty my mouth felt like I'd been eating sand and to top it off the taste of my own blood was awful. I knew I'd been in that fucking trunk for more than an hour and the car had finally come to a stop. Where the fuck was I? I was hearing voices, and then the car doors slammed. "The bitch is in the trunk claiming she doesn't know where the money is, so I say instead of killing her silly ass, we torture her until she confesses," Lo said. Oh my God torture? I began to cry even though no one could hear me due to my damn mouth being duct taped and gagged. I would rather those motherfuckers just killed me and took me out of my misery. I honestly didn't know what fucking money he talking about. For all I knew Ray and Santana weren't on good terms.

"Get the bitch Lo," I heard somebody say but it wasn't Santana. The trunk opened and Lo grabbed me by my ankles dragging me out the trunk as if I was already dead. My head was bouncing like a ball and my body felt like it was filled with needles when it hit the ground. They really were trying to make me suffer. Laughing, the unknown man said, "Damn Lo you act like the bitch stole from you, you could at least pick the bitch up and make her hop."

"Man fuck this hoe! She did steal from me, she's the reason why my father wasn't in my life and the reason I killed my dumb ass mother," Lo said sounding angrier. So he blamed me for Ray not being there and maybe he blamed Mona too. But wait, Linda said that Lo didn't know, and why was he blaming me for him killing Linda? "Ray was a grown ass man Lo, and believe it or not he was there for you. You just didn't know it," the unknown voice spoke again.

"Let's get this raggedy hoe in the spot and get down to business," said Lo. At that point, the way he was handling me I'd rather have taken a bullet to the head over that shit. "Stand her up and let her hop her ass in," Santana said. Now I was standing and hopping because my ankles were tied together. It seemed like I was moving in slow motion and there was rocks or gravel of some sort under my feet. They must have had my ass in the middle of nowhere. It was the kind shit you saw on movies or read about in those street novels. "Ok this is it," I heard the voice say then a door opened. "Sit down," Santana said and pushed me down in a chair that was so cold it sent a chill up my spine and made my teeth chatter. It must have been metal and sitting in a damn freezer or something. He removed the blindfold from my eyes and the light burned them. I blinked a few times trying to get my eyes adjusted to the light. I wanted so desperately to see who that voice belonged to, and when I opened my eyes, I thought I was seeing a ghost. It looked like my husband.

My eyes began to water and he removed the tape and cloth that was used to gag me. He looked a little aged and like he had maybe gained a few pounds, but I was almost sure it was him. "R-r-r ray," I said looking baffled. The three of them burst out laughing. "I'm confused," I said. "You really are a delusional bitch aren't you?" the Ray look-alike asked. "Ah you may or may not have had knowledge of me, but I'm Armando Ramirez, Ray's father," he said with a smile. "But you look identical to him," I said. "Yeah well look around at the men in this room, we all look alike. The genes are strong dear."

I looked at him, Santana, and Lo, and exactly as he

said, they all looked alike. "Ray never spoke of you. I knew he had a father but I never knew you were a part of his life," I said, confused yet again. "Well to my understanding Ray didn't tell you much of shit," he said with a laugh, "So you see you're here because my son had some money that belonged to me and I want it." He looked at me in a way that immediately made me feel uncomfortable. "I'm going to tell you the same thing I told that mother fucker," I said looking at Santana. "I don't know about no money." He smiled a half-smile and clapped his hands together. "I gave you a chance, a way out per say, but you seem to be too stubborn. It's ok though. I understand, but I need you to understand something about me and that is I simply don't give a fuck about you and for that reason alone you are going to have to die."

He turned and walked away. I noticed there was a long table in the corner filled with all types of guns. "What the fuck are those crazy niggas planning to do," I thought. I was lost in thought about Ray again. "Ray what you have gotten me into? You hurt me while you were alive and now beyond the grave." I was sitting there feeling like my whole body was numb. I guess what they say about karma being a bitch was true and that must have been my karma. I realized they hadn't mentioned Mona. Oh God, what had they done to my child? "Wait," I yelled.

Armando turned around. "Where is Mona? What have you done to my daughter? If you hurt her I swear." He cut me off and said, "You're in no position to ask questions or make threats bitch. However, since you won't be seeing her ever again it's safe to say my granddaughter is fine and she will be fine. She got away but it isn't in my interest to hurt her. She's just a lost child who endured abuse at the hands of the one who was supposed to protect her. That alone has signed your death certificate."

That time all three of them left the room closing and locking the door leaving me alone with my own guilt and thoughts. I didn't realize it until then but it was cold in that motherfucker. "Where the fuck am I?" I thought. "I'm sorry baby girl," I spoke as if Mona could hear me. "I'm guilty of abuse and putting my only child out in the street to prostitute herself. I'm guilty of setting my husband up to be robbed and ultimately leading to him being killed." I hadn't had a relationship with my own mother since Mona was born. I was just a fucked up individual. As I was sitting there not

Roni J.

knowing if I was going to see my daughter again. I felt like I deserve to die for all that I put her through. If I got the chance, I would fix it. "I just have to," I thought as I felt myself getting sleepy.

A Daughters Rage

Kevin

That shit had gone too far and I needed answers. I had to go and visit Vanessa Brown my birth mother. Visiting hours were over at 8 pm and looking at the time, I only had about 45 minutes to get to Sheppard Pratt and less than that to question her. All I needed was 10 minutes for her to tell me something, anything that was going to make that shit make sense to me. "Hold tight lil mama I'm coming. I just need to find out something that could possibly help us both," I said to myself as I thought about Mona.

Sheppard Pratt Mental Facility

Pulling up in the facility parking lot my stomach was doing flips but I couldn't back out now that I was there. I had questions, and I wanted answers. Parking my car, I turned off the engine and got out staring at the building that looked like a fancy ass jailhouse. I made my way to the glass sliding doors, and walked through them to the front desk.

"May I help you sir?" the young white girl sitting

at the desk asked. "Yes I'm here to see Vanessa Brown." She punched keys on her computer keyboard. "And your name sir?" she asked looking up at me then back at her computer. By her facial expression, I felt that if I told her my name she wouldn't see me on the list. If there was even one because nobody went to see Ness. "Uh yes my name is Kevin Jones," I said. "Ok Mr. Jones visiting hours are over in 30 minutes," she said with a smile. Shockingly Vanessa had me listed; she must have known someday I would have questions that needed answers. "Here place this sticker on your shirt, take the first elevator to the third floor, and go to the right to the first nurse's station. They'll handle it from there," she said smiling at me and indirectly flirting. I smiled back and told her, "Thanks." She just simply nodded her head.

A Daughters Rage

Mona

I jumped up realizing I had gone to sleep unintentionally. Where the fuck was Kevin? It was almost 8 o'clock. It didn't take over an hour to get a damn chicken box. I was beyond angry and I was starving. I couldn't sit there like a bump on a log waiting for him to come. I needed to get the hell out of there. The True Religion jeans I was wearing were tight and my belly top was showing my flat stomach. My ass was round and phat and my titties were firm and perky. I didn't look like the average 14 year old. I guess my body was forced to develop since I'd been fucking grown men for the past 2 years. I decided not to put my coat on but looking down at my all white Polo socks, I thought, "Got damn I need some shoes." I was in survival mode as I left the room headed to the front desk. I was going to eat whether Kevin came or not. Sticking my head out the door I spotted a potential trick leaned up against a black Lexus truck. How the fuck was I supposed to approach that man in a pair of fucking socks that looked like I'd been walking through mud all day. I laughed. "What the fuck," I thought. I was getting angry. He had his head down doing something on his phone but when I

Roni J.

opened my mouth, he looked up.

"Hey you," I yelled. He looked confused and began to look around. My stomach growled. I hoped he didn't hear that shit. He looked up at me and asked, "Are you talking to me?" I nodded. He smiled. I got straight to the point. "Look by the why you're looking at me I know you know exactly what I'm thinking. I don't have time for small talk so let's get straight to the point." He raised his brow and frowned.

"You should never judge a book by its cover little girl. You're inexperienced. You see I'm a grown ass man with a big ass dick that would bust your little ass open from a to z. You're barking up the wrong tree youngster so I suggest you prance your little hot ass on before you get what you don't need." He laughed and continued looking at his phone. Damn his rudeness had my pussy pulsating. He had shit all wrong. I could fuck and suck him like no other. I continued to push. Now I was horny on top of being hungry.

"See that's where you're wrong. You should never judge a book by its cover, you're right about one thing, and that is the fact that I'm young. But I would fuck the shit out of you old head." He started laughing. "I warned you but you seem to want this dick. At what cost?" He was no longer smiling and his face became very serious. "Got damn I'm cold," I thought. "I tell you what. I'm so confident that you'll enjoy me you figure it out and by the time we're done you'll change your mind," I giggled. He began to grab his dick through his pants. I hoped he didn't want to go back to my room. I couldn't risk Kevin coming in on us. "Ok let's go," he said smiling.

I walked around the desk and followed him to the back where there was a small but cozy room. "He must live here," I thought. "Ok show me what you're working with," he said with a raised eyebrow. Moving close to him and grabbing the waistline of his sweats, I could see his dick print through his pants and it was huge. I began to pull his pants down until they fell around his ankles. "Damn this motherfucker got a big ass dick," I thought. Looking at his dick, I saw that it was long and thick. The head was the size of a huge mushroom and it had a vein that was shaped like a bolt of lightning, directly in the center. As I continued to admire that juicy oversized dick, my pussy was leaking, and my juices were starting to seep through my panties.

Roni J.

"What are you waiting for youngster? You scared?" he asked. I sat on the bed and pulled him to me. Right hand on his shaft and left hand on his balls, I wrapped my full wet lips around the head of his dick; flicking my tongue over the hole in a slow circular motion while gently massaging his balls. They felt heavy. He was moaning a little. I popped the head out of my mouth as if it was a lollipop; he grabbed my head and said, "Fuck all that! Suck this motherfucker!" I did as I was told. I spit on the dick and slowly took it in my mouth inch-by-inch, sucking, and deep throating. I felt his dick throbbing so I sped up taking the whole 11 inches in my mouth. I knew it was 11 inches because that's the most I was able to deep throat thus far with no gag reflex.

"No I'm not ready to come yet. Give me that pussy," he said growling. I quickly got undressed and lay back on the bed. I opened my legs wide exposing my bald, phat, pink pussy. I slowly stuck my pointer and middle finger in my pussy stroking slowly in and out. "Mm mm," I moaned while looking at him. I took my fingers out and sucked my own juices.

Watching me finger fuck myself was driving him crazy. He grabbed a condom, rolled it on, and flipped me over. "Dammit," I thought. I was now on my knees, ass in the air, and my back arched. He used two fingers to separate my pussy lips as he entered me slowly. I felt the width of his dick opening me up; as he pushed his dick in inch-by-inch, he began to grunt. "Damn youngster this pussy tight and juicy as a motherfucker," he said while stroking. His strokes got deeper and I felt my orgasm reaching my clitoris. "Hmmmmm," I was moaning as he sped up. Oh my God, I'd never felt anything like that before. He was pumping me harder and I was cumming again and again. My legs were shaking uncontrollably. I couldn't stop cumming and I yelled out, "Yes oh my God yes! Please don't stop!" I didn't know if I wanted him to stop or not but what I did know was I felt like I was about to pass the fuck out. I most definitely was not prepared for that shit. I thought I might have to holler at that nigga again. I looked back at him while my ass bounced off his balls.

He pumped harder and I came again. I couldn't take it anymore. I felt dizzy; that nigga was literally fucking the dog shit out of me. He stuck his thumb in my ass, grabbed the back of my neck, squeezed, and as weird as it might seem, I loved that kinky shit. "Ahh... mm... mm... got

Roni J.

damn," he was moaning and cumming at the same damn time. I collapsed on the bed face down, sweating and hungry as a slave. "Get dressed," he said walking into the bathroom. I was confused, was he going to pay me or tell me to leave? I'd been in that type of situation before so I jumped up and got dressed quickly.

By the time he came out of the bathroom I was ready to go and he handed me a $100 bill. "You earned that youngster," he said smiling. I smirked. "Oh yeah, well thanks," I said. Shit, I was relieved. I thought that nigga was about to play me. "Here's my number, holler at me," he said giving me a piece of paper. "Maybe I will or maybe I won't," I said turning to leave and stuffing the number in my pocket. I was so caught up in my own thoughts that I didn't see the guy in the hoodie standing at the desk. It didn't matter. I was out the door headed to McDonald's across the street. It was 8:30. I didn't know if Kevin came back to the room or not but at that point, I didn't even give a fuck. I was going to eat, shower, and get ready for my meeting with Heads. I really hoped he didn't turn me away.

Jogging across the street and walking into McDonald's, I noticed the bitch at the register from my school. She immediately had attitude written all over her face. I hoped I didn't have to smack that bitch. I just wanted to get my food and leave. Realizing my ass was barefoot, I got an attitude, but I was trying my best to play it off since I was the only customer in the store. "Can I get a Big Mac meal, super-sized with a Coke, and an apple pie?" I asked. The bitch looked at me as if I had shit on my face and asked, "Is that all?" I looked at her and said, "Ain't that all I ordered?" I tapped my fingertips on the counter. "Bitch," I thought. After she rung up my food and I got my change I headed back to my room and in the process, I caught a glimpse of the dude in the hoodie leaving the motel. It was Heads but he didn't see me. What was he doing there and what was the connection with him and dude? "Damn I wonder where he's going. Shit," I thought. It would be 9 o'clock soon. I had an hour and then I was making my move without Kevin's ass. I shook my head sitting down on the side of the dirty ass bed to eat my food.

Roni J.

A Daughters Rage

Kevin

I was standing in the doorway of her room just staring at Vanessa. She was sitting in a chair staring out the window; her hair was long and silky. "Ness, I mean Ma," I said. It sounded weird coming out of my mouth but it was my reality. She was my birth mother. Without turning around she spoke. "Kevin, I knew this day would come when you would be demanding answers and I'm prepared to answer whatever you want and need to know," she said still staring out the window. I was speechless. That was easier than I thought. "I have so many questions," I said.

"Ok let's do it this way," she said and turned around to face me. "I'll talk and you'll listen. I promise by the time I'm done you'll have all the answers you're looking for."

"Ok," I said. She started to talk. "Sandy and I used to be best friends back in the day before Ray came in the picture. Ray was the main dealer in the hood and every hot ass teenage girl including myself was after him. He took advantage of that by sleeping with us all. Me, Linda, Laverne, Sandy, and a few others." She looked at me I nodded my head so she could continue.

"Ray and Sandy got together as a couple our last year of high school. I got depressed not because I wanted him, but because I knew what type of guy Ray was. We all did, except Sandy. She was naive and still a virgin. Ray was everything to her. I stopped fucking Ray out of guilt, he was with my best friend and I couldn't do it no more. I was truly starting to catch feelings for him and to this day Sandy still doesn't know about Ray and me. To take the attention off of me I told Sandy about Linda and Ray. They were still together while he was with Sandy. He refused to leave Linda alone and she was ok with being the other woman. They were still messing around when Lo killed her. Lo never knew Ray was his father because Linda was fucking another guy named Light Skin Mac, but Lo wasn't stupid. He was starting to put shit together and Sandy popping up at their house only confirmed what he was thinking. The day Lo snapped and killed Linda and his little brother Mac was the day she told him Ray was his father." She stopped talking and she looked at me. I was stunned and I knew it was written all over my face. "Kevin you ok baby?" she asked.

A Daughters Rage

"Hold up! What the fuck? So Lo knows that Mona is his sister?" I asked. "I'm fucked up mentally," I thought. "Yes he knows and he hates her. He blames Mona and Sandy for Ray not being there for him, but truth is Ray was there almost every day. He paid Linda's bills and dressed Lo in the most updated clothing and sneakers, but he didn't want Lo to know that he was his father yet because he knew Lo wouldn't understand," she said looking as if she was about to break down. "All this time he knew Mona was his sister and he was thinking of her in a sexual way. Not for enjoyment, but out of pure hate. He wants to hurt her," she said still talking and I felt like I was about to lose it.

"Are you ok Kevin?" she asked again. "Um yeah I'm just trying to grasp all of what you're telling me," I said. "When I first found out Linda was pregnant I was jealous, hurt, and angry because a part of me wanted it to be me. Also because I was questioning why Linda would do that to Sandy and I was planning to confront her and Ray about it. The day I decided to confront them, Ray stopped by my house to tell me not to say a word about Linda being pregnant. My feelings came rushing back and I allowed him to seduce me. We fucked right there on the floor," she explained looking disappointed. I looked at her like she was fucking crazy; I mean she was, that's why she was there. "Why would you do that?" I asked. "Truth is I don't know Kevin. Young and dumb I guess. I was beginning to feel like that would happen every time Ray and I came in contact so I decided to move to DC away from it all. Sandy didn't want me to go, but I had to," she continued. My mind was in overdrive. My heart was beating so fast and hard it was as if I had a drum in my damn chest. I was starting to sweat. I knew she was not about to tell me what the fuck I thought she was. "DC. I'm from DC," I yelled jumping straight to the point.

"Ma, was Ray my father too?" I asked. She was staring at me with watery eyes, and I didn't need her to answer. She didn't have to say it. Her expression told all. "The part that hurts the most is I never got a chance to know him," I said. I felt my eyes watering. "I found out I was pregnant about 2 months after I moved to DC. I was hurt and confused; I didn't know what to do, so I never even told Ray I was pregnant. I stayed in DC until after I had you. I knew I was going back to Baltimore and the fact that you looked like Ray would have made it easy for him to put it together that you were also his son. I couldn't do that to Sandy. My truth ate away at my mind so I gave you up for adoption. Giving you up is how I started getting high. I couldn't believe that I gave my baby up to keep from hurting someone else," she said crying. I was trying to understand everything. My eyes began to water, I felt the tears about to fall, and I let them. "Now I know why I have this feeling of obligation to Mona. She's my sister, and Lo is my brother. This is some twisted shit," I thought.

"So all those times when you were helping me and looking out for me it was your way of being in my life unbeknownst to me?" I asked. She looked at me and said, "Yes, and after I tell you this you're probably going to hate me, but I have to tell you this."

I was thinking, "You just dropped the bomb on me. What could be worse than that?"

"There's more?" I asked. "Yes there is. Please let me finish while I have the nerve to," she said wiping her face with the back of her hand. "Ok I'm listening," I said after taking a deep breath. "One day Sandy called my mother's house crying and upset talking about how Ray was still cheating on her and that he was Lo's father. I knew that already but I acted surprised. She said she was tired and wanted to teach him a lesson so that's where I came in. She knew I was getting high and that I knew a lot of street niggas so she wanted me to orchestrate Ray getting robbed. I told her I would do it but I was scared so I told her I'd get back to her," she said.

She must've noticed the look on my face because she stopped. I looked at her, she began talking, and everything seemed to be moving in slow motion. "I knew this young dude who was friends with Lo and I presented the robbery idea to him and he told Lo. Lo got back to me and said he'd do it and that he was going to holler at one of his boys to drive the getaway car. I didn't know that the homeboy he was talking about was you."

She didn't even have to say any more. I was an accessory to my own father's murder. I didn't pull the trigger, but I was driving the car. I couldn't believe this. "I have to get the fuck out of here," I thought.

I stood to leave, looked at my mother, I was crying and so was she. I walked away without saying a word and she didn't even try to stop me. My balance was off. On my way to the elevator, I bumped into someone, but I wasn't paying attention. I was crying so hard my vision was blurred. First I found out I was adopted, then all in one breath I was told that my birth mother used me and my brother who I didn't even know was my brother, to kill my father that I never knew. And that I had a sister. What kind of shit was that? I wanted answers and I for damn sure got them, but I wished I didn't. I was so upset I didn't even realize that I was sitting in my car. I didn't even remember getting to my car. I was distraught and overwhelmed. I was crying so hard that I felt sick. Maybe I just needed to sit there for a minute before I went see Mona. "How do I explain this to her?" I asked myself. Fuck looking for Sandy. I needed to find a way to explain all of that shit to my sister. I wiped my face on the sleeve of my hoodie and started the car.

As I was driving, my hands were shaking on the steering wheel. I was nervous Mona wouldn't understand. Shit, I didn't even understand myself. I was so deep in my thoughts I didn't realize I'd run a red light. "When did I even start my damn car?" I thought. The sound of horns blowing, tires screeching, and then a loud crash was all that registered before everything went

Roni J.

black.

A Daughters Rage

Vanessa

I knew that Kevin would come to me with questions once I told him I was his birth mother. I was already mentally unstable and on suicide watch as it was, and I was feeling like my time here on earth was up. When I found out I was HIV positive I knew my life was over. That was why I tried to slit my wrist. So that I could join the devil. I mean he was my best friend; he was the reason for my life turning out to be so fucked up. I had been expecting Kevin to come to me before then. I'd been waiting for that moment for the past year, and now that it had come, I had to follow through. I hadn't planned on one of the nurses leaving a pair of scissors on the desk the other day during recreation time and I took that as a sign from God that it was my time to go. As soon as she stepped away to help a patient I swiped them, took them in my room, and hid them. I'd been occasionally sharpening them on the windowsill in my room. Since it was made of concrete, it was easy to sharpen them enough to cut into the flesh on my wrist. I sat there writing my final words to Kevin in a letter. I was sure it was what I wanted to do.

Roni J.

The Letter

Kevin;

My precious baby, my son, my one, and only love. By the time you read this, I will be in the only place that's suitable for people like me. I never meant to hurt you. I was only trying to protect you from the drama and lies that would've had you fucked up as a child. I still failed because now you know everything, but you're old enough to deal with it better. I want you to be there for your sister and please find it in your heart to forgive me. I don't want you to feel like it's your fault that your father is gone because it's not. It was Lo who killed Ray. The day that I went to Lo with the proposition to rob Ray it was out of anger. When I told Ray that you were his son, he called me a lying, jealous, junkie bitch. I knew Lo hated him so I went to him with it, but I swear to you I didn't know he was going to kill him. Take care of yourself and your baby sister son and try your best to walk away from the street life. It's not for you. You have so much potential, potential to be great. I love you, I've always loved you, and now it's time for me to go. I don't want a funeral; I would like to be cremated. My mother has an insurance policy on me that she took out when she found out I was

A Daughters Rage

getting high off drugs and had contracted HIV. The money is yours. Use it to start over. You can reach out to my mother. She knows about you and she wants to meet you. Her address is 1634 Carswell Street. Her number is 676-555-8209. Call her baby. I love you son.

I folded the letter and wrote, "To my son," on the outside. I hoped that whoever found it would get it to Kevin. I placed it on my pillow, went into my bathroom, and sat on the toilet with the scissors in my right hand. I slowly slid the sharpest part across my wrist. It broke the skin but not deep enough to cause any damage so I repeatedly went over that same spot again. It burned like hell and I watched as my blood leaked from my body. At first, it was pouring out onto the floor rapidly, and then it started to drip. I was beginning to feel lightheaded, my eyes started to flutter, and my heart rate started slowing down. I knew no one would find me until morning because our nightly count had just been completed. I slowly started to lose my balance and fell over on the floor. I thought I was ready to face death head on, but as my life began to flash before my eyes and I stared at the ceiling. I was feeling like I may have made the wrong decision to commit suicide. It was too

Roni J.

late though and I closed my eyes forever.

A Daughters Rage

Mona

Damn I was hungry; I devoured my food in less than five minutes. I laughed to myself, greedy ass. I loved food. Kevin still hadn't come back but it was ok. I wasn't tripping. I was about to shower and get ready to meet Heads. It was a damn shame I didn't have any clean underwear or a change of clothes. I really didn't want to shower and put on the same saturated ass panties that I put on after I fucked dude so I decided I just wouldn't wear any at all.

After I was done showering, I'd call Mya, and then take a cab to Head's house. Damn those towels looked dirty as shit but they smelled clean so I used them. I put one in the tub because I refused to put my bare feet in that rusty looking tub. As soon as I turned the water on the shit was brown. "Oh my God what the fuck is next? Damn," I said yelling. After a while, the water started to clear up but it was cold as ice. "Where the fuck is the hot water?" I asked myself looking around. I spotted a bar of unopened soap on the side of the tub. It didn't have a name on it. The shit might break me out but I was in no position to be picky. I

Roni J.

grabbed the soap to open it and it crumbled in my damn hand. "What the fuck?" I yelled. "How old is this shit, is it stale," I thought.

I ran the water on it to make suds and it worked so instead of using the washcloth, I used my hands to lather the soap up over my body and between my legs trying not to put any inside my pussy. I was in fear of getting a bad infection of some sort. That was one thing Sandy's bitch ass taught me how to do. That was to be clean and that your pussy was one of the most sensitive places on your body. I wondered what Heads was going to say when I just popped up at his house.

Turning the water off and stepping out of the shower I thought I heard a door shut so I peeked my head out of the bathroom. I didn't see anybody. "Maybe it's my nerves," I thought. My birthday was coming up and my life was fucked up. I was kidnapped, tied up, and forced to suck Lo's funky ass dick. Then I was rescued by Kevin and now I was in hiding in a broke down ass, rat hole, of a motel. That shit was crazy. I needed to go visit my daddy. Maybe I'd go to his gravesite on my birthday.

"Knock! Knock!" I heard a knock on the

door. "It must be Kevin," I thought. "Hold on I'm coming," I yelled. I walked to the door wrapping the towel around my wet body. I was about to cuss his slow ass out. I reached for the knob and swung the door open turning my back on him. "Damn Kevin what the fuck? Did you have to kill the chicken?" I asked. The voice that answered froze me in my tracks and I couldn't move. It wasn't Kevin and I panicked. My heart felt like it was about to jump out of my damn chest but before I could try and run the voice spoke and said, "You should never open a door without asking who it is first. Sorry to disappoint you but I'm not Kevin and word on the street is you're looking for me." I still hadn't turned around yet. "Um who are you and why would I be looking for you?" I asked my voice trembling and still not turning around.

"I go by Heads," he said. I almost jumped out my damn skin. "Go ahead and get dressed. I'll wait," he said. Damn how did he know I was there? Did he see me when I left earlier? His cousin must've told him I was asking questions about him. Damn I was all over the place in my thoughts. I was in the bathroom putting my clothes back on. I was nervous and shaking. Shit I had it all planned out, what I was going to say, but now I could barely breathe. Fuck! "I'll be out in just a minute," I yelled. He didn't say anything. I checked myself out in the mirror. I thought my nerves were getting the best of me because I was beginning to sweat. "Got dammit Monie get your shit together," I said to myself.

I opened the door and he was leaning up against the wall. Damn he was sexy. I felt my pussy tingle all over again. "So," he said. I couldn't let him see how nervous I was so I acted real nonchalant. "So the word is right, I am looking for you. I'm in some shit, and my father told me if I was ever in any trouble that you'd look out for me. So you need to handle that," I said with an attitude. He laughed, and seemed unfazed by my smart-ass mouth. "Are you done little girl?" he asked. So he saw me as nothing but a child. I was hurt, so I didn't say shit. He continued. "As I thought. First, let me clarify some shit for you. I don't owe you shit; your father was like a father to me. He practically raised me off those streets and if it wasn't for him, I would probably be dead already. I made a promise to him that if something ever happened to him that I would look after you and make sure you never needed anything. Out of respect for him, I'll do just that. Second, you need to check your funky ass attitude because although I love and respect Ray

A Daughters Rage

beyond the grave, I won't do shit and leave you assed out," he yelled. "Do I make myself clear," he said with a serious look on his face. After all that he just said, all I could do was say, "Yes."

"Good now tell me what's going on," he said calmly.

Roni J.

A Daughters Rage

University Hospital Shock/Trauma Unit

Kevin was flown via helicopter to University of Maryland shock/trauma. His car had collided with a big rig when he ran the red light. Both of his legs, arms, and several ribs were broken. He suffered from a temporal brain trauma. The doctors were doing everything they could to keep him stabilized. However, he kept flat lining. Hours passed and he was finally stable, but he was in a coma in the ICU.

"For some reason I feel that all this shit is linked," Jake said. "Yeah I'm thinking the same thing. It was not a coincidence that Lorenzo and Santana both were at Sandy's house and left basically dragging her ass out the door," Romello said. "I knew that bitch knew more than what she was telling us, and now they have her. Mona is somewhere, but where? Lu said Mya told her that Mona was with Kevin but she wasn't in that car. I just hope Lucille calls me when Mona contacts Mya again. I wonder what Armando wanted with her anyway," Jake said. "Well she is his granddaughter J," Romello said.

"Yeah you have a point." He laughed. "Well

since it doesn't look like Kevin will be going anywhere anytime soon, we'll just have to tell him when he wakes up that Vanessa's crazy ass done killed herself. Maybe he knows something that we should since he visited her an hour before she committed suicide." He laughed again.

"You ain't shit J; all this shit is funny to you." Romello laughed as well. "Yeah it is funny watching these motherfuckers go through all this wild shit. It makes me sleep better at night knowing somebody else's life is so fucked up that it makes mine seem like a fairy tale." Romello shook his head. "I guess you're right, so are we hooking up tonight, or are you going to be fucking your wife while thinking about me?" he asked.

"Yes we are hooking up. I need to bust that tight ass baby," Jake said smiling. "Ok. I'll be glad when you finally leave that skinny bitch and come home where you belong," Romello responded. "Shhh! here comes the doc," Jake said and Romello rolled his eyes.

"Ok Officers, Mr. Jones is in a coma but if anything changes with his condition, or if someone comes to visit him we'll be sure to contact you. Now if there isn't anything else I need to get back to work," she said looking down at her clipboard.

"Ok doc we were just leaving, you have a good rest of the night Ma'am," Jake said. "Will do," she said.

Romello pressed the button to bring the elevator up. "Ding!" The elevator sounded and the doors opened. They both stepped on. "You have to stop being so loud when we're out in public Mello. She could've easily heard you," Jake said with an attitude. Romello smacked his teeth and said, "Whatever. I'm done with this shit. I'll see you later or maybe I won't." Jake grabbed his dick through his pants and said, "Oh you will see me later."

"Ding!" The elevator sounded again indicating they'd reached the lobby. The doors opened and they both stepped off. Once in the lobby they went their separate ways without saying another word.

Roni J.

A Daughters Rage

Armando's Warehouse

The warehouse looked shabby and run down on the outside. That was part of the cover up. On the inside, it was huge and spacious with three levels. A large 62-inch flat screen television was mounted to the wall with the evening news on. The anchorman was talking about the terrible car accident that Kevin had been in. A huge oak desk sat in the center of the floor with a soft leather swivel chair behind it. "I told them fucking fags to bring me my granddaughter. What the fuck is the problem," Armando yelled pacing back and forth. "Pop they must've not found her yet. She wasn't in the car with Kevin, and so she could be anywhere," Santana said wondering the same thing. "Where the Fuck is Lo's unstable ass? He thinks I don't know what the fuck he did but I do, and I'm going to make him suffer for it. Little sick fucker! She's his sister. If he didn't look like us I wouldn't believe he had our blood running through his veins, but that's already been confirmed as well," Armando yelled angrily. Santana laughed and he had a thought. "Have you spoken to Momma? You know Ray was her pride and joy. She may know where that money is Pops," Santana said.

Roni J.

"Your mother loved herself some Ray, but she never approved of this lifestyle and refused to involve herself in anything illegal. I know she doesn't know anything," Armando responded. Selma Ramirez was the daughter of Felipe Santiago, a well-known drug lord that ran the Santiago cartel down in Mexico back in the early 80's. However, the beef her family constantly had with the Lucas cartel had gotten her mother killed. After losing her mother Selma vowed to never involve herself in the family business. To that day, she had kept her word even though her spot as head of the family was and always would be available if she ever changed her mind. Lo walked in the room and they both looked at him. He was sweating and his white shirt was off and thrown over his shoulder. It had blood on it. "What the fuck did you do?" Armando asked yelling.

"I took dat bitch's ass, that's what I did old man," Lo said without blinking. Santana just stood there with a shocked expression on his face. At that moment, Armando thought back to what Lo did to Mona and all his anger came rushing back. He charged at Lo full force knocking him off his feet and causing him to hit his head on the corner of one of the wood pallets that was neatly stacked.

A Daughters Rage

"Pop," Santana yelled. Armando was on top of Lo with his hand around his throat. "We don't rape women," Armando said yelling. "He's going too far," Armando continued calming down a little. "Ok Pop let him go before you kill the lil nigga," Santana yelled grabbing Armando. Neither of them noticed that Lo wasn't moving. When he hit his head, the impact had knocked him out.

"Enough is enough. This shit ain't right, I threatened Sandy as a scare tactic, you and I both know that," Armando said while letting go of Lo and standing up. Santana noticed that Lo wasn't moving. "Oh shit Pop, what did you do? He ain't moving," Santana said nervously. "I… I didn't do shit because you stopped me, what the fuck you mean he not moving?" Armando asked nervously. Then he saw the small blood puddle on the floor behind his head. "What the fuck," Armando yelled. "Pop we've got to get him to a hospital, his heart is still beating. I think he hit his head when you dived on him." Lo was unconscious but breathing.

"Ok let's get him in the truck. Where's the closest hospital?" asked Armando. "From here I think it's Franklin Square up in Rosedale," Santana said. "Shit, ok let's go. Get his legs and I'll get his upper body," Armando said putting his arms under

Roni J.

Lo's armpits. Santana did the same to his legs and they carried him out to Armando's Cadillac truck. Laying him across the back seat, they both shut the doors and hopped in the truck. Santana drove. Fifteen minutes later, they arrived at Franklin Square ER.

Santana jumped out of the truck and busted through the Emergency Room doors yelling. "We need a doctor, my nephew fell and hit his head. He's bleeding and I think he's unconscious," he yelled. "Where's the child sir?" a doctor asked. "He's not a child and he's in the truck right outside the door," Santana said sounding a little nervous. "Ok get me a gurney," the doctor yelled as she ran out the door to the truck. She immediately started asking questions. "How old is the patient? How did this happen? Where did this happen?"

"He's 19 and it happened when he slipped and fell out at the warehouse lifting some boxes," Santana explained letting the lie roll off his tongue naturally. Armando looked at him totally confused. He wasn't a liar, and even though he understood why he lied, he still didn't agree with it. He went along with it anyway. The doctor had a look of skepticism etched on her face. "Ok first we have to stop the bleeding," she said. Lo was way over the alcohol limit for someone of his weight and height so when he hit his head the alcohol made him bleed more.

"It's not as bad as it looks; he had a small gash, more like a puncture. He must've hit his head on some sort of sharp object, and the alcohol intensified the bleeding causing him to pass out. A few stitches and some pain meds and he'll be fine," the doc informed them.

"How do you know that he's been drinking doc," Santana asked. "Because I can smell it on his breath," she said. Both Armando and Santana breathed a sigh of relief. Santana because he was out on parole and would rather die before going back to jail. Surely, that would be the case if Lo had died. Armando because he wasn't trying to bring Lo harm, not at the moment anyway. He had questions for him that needed answers. They sat in the waiting area waiting for the doctor to return with an update on Lorenzo's condition. About thirty minutes later Doctor Julia Monroe returned.

"Allow me to introduce myself as I didn't get a chance to do so before. Helping your nephew was my first priority. My name is Dr. Julia Monroe and I'm happy to inform you that Lorenzo is stable and we've stopped the bleeding. He has ten stitches and is sleeping right now. We want to keep him overnight for observation, but ultimately he's going to be ok," she said confidently. "Ok doc," was all Armando said before he and Santana both left.

A Daughters Rage

Sandy

"Just fucking kill me already," I yelled crying. "The pain is overbearing. I can barely move. I guess I deserve this for what I've done to you," I said speaking to Ray as if he was standing right there in front of me. I lay there helplessly, while Lo shoved his dick in my ass. I felt my anus ripping apart and I couldn't move. I couldn't scream. I couldn't do shit. I'd never felt that kind of pain in my life and as I lay there on that cold ass concrete floor I thought about Mona and what he might have done to her, my baby girl, my only child. I felt sick, and guilt started to set in. I treated her so badly. Was I jealous of my own child? The attention she got from Ray. He was always so concerned about her and what was best for her. He never seemed to care about how I felt about the whores he was fucking outside of me. How could any woman be content with being the whore on the side? It was fucking absurd.

Linda deserved to die for what she and Ray put me through. Vanessa thought I don't know that she was fucking Ray but I'd known about her and Laverne. Ray told me about them himself and I let

Roni J.

it go for two reasons. One being I knew they both were whores and two he was honest. I believed him when he told me it was a onetime thing. I was also convinced that Kevin might be his son as well. The resemblance was uncanny. I never told Kevin about that, but I felt him being so worried about Mona was too much like the way Ray used to be. When and if I get through this, I would get to the bottom of it and find out who Kevin really was. I had to find a way to get out of there. I couldn't die like that. I looked up and began praying. "Lord I know I've fucked up with you but if you can please spare me so I can get out and find my baby girl I promise I won't let you down."

A Daughters Rage

Mona

That shit with Heads was not going to be as easy as I thought it would be. He too moody and quick tempered. "I bet he can fuck to, hmmmm," I thought. "I'm waiting," he said with his eyebrow raised. I realized I was staring. "Oh yeah, so earlier today I'm at Shake and Bake skate rink with my best friend Mya and her mom. We were tired and decided to leave. While they were in the bathroom I was sitting on the bench taking my skates off when Lo came up behind me, touched my shoulder and said, 'You either going to go by choice or by force but either way you're going.' I didn't want anybody to get hurt because of me so I went with him. He took me to a house over on Martin Luther King Blvd., tied me up, gagged my mouth with duct tape, and put me in the basement. I remember the house; I've seen it before. I was confused because I didn't know what the fuck he was going to do," I said. Heads was looking at me as if he didn't believe me and then he said, "I've got to get you out of here so let's go."

"What the fuck," I thought. I looked around the room making sure I was not leaving shit

123

Roni J.

behind. I grabbed my coat and we walked out to his car. Heads had an all silver Chevy Impala. That mother was fresh. Looked like he just drove it off the lot. He unlocked the door, opened the passenger side for me to get in, and then he walked around to the driver's side and got in himself. It had that fresh new car scent. The white leather seats were as soft as a baby's ass and the stereo system was the shit. "Yeah this nigga making bank," I thought.

"So let me get this straight, this nigga just came into the rink, grabbed you up kidnapping you, and you don't know why?" he asked with a frown on his face. "No the fuck I don't," I yelled. "I know the nigga is crazy and I try my best to stay the fuck out of his path, so how would I know." I snapped. I was truly pissed off and agitated that this motherfucker was really playing with me. "I'm only going to say this one more time. You need to watch who the fuck you talking to. I'm the wrong nigga. I'm trying to make some sense of this bullshit," he yelled.

"Did he really just refer to my situation as bullshit? Fuck this shit! I'm not dealing with this arrogant ass motherfucker," I thought. "You know what? Fuck all this shit I'll figure it out on my own or they'll just kill my ass. Either way I'm not dealing with this shit from you," I said yelling.

Heads was looking at me like I was crazy "You really do have a smart ass mouth little girl, but I won't say it again. You're the one who needs me so that whole lil fire cracker thing you got going on you can kill that shit," he said laughing.

"There's more so continue," he said. I was looking at that crazy motherfucker as if he'd lost his damn mind. In a way I was kind of glad he didn't put my ass out. I was anxious to know where we were going so I decided to finish telling him. "As I was saying, he kept asking me about this money and he really expected me to know. Even if I did, I couldn't speak with a dirty ass rag down my throat and my mouth taped up. He started getting angrier by the minute so he decided that he wanted his dick sucked. So of course, he wanted me to do that too. He pulled his pants down just below his ass, pulled out his fishy smelling dick, ungagged me, and put it in my mouth." The thought of it made me gag. "Anyway, I told him I didn't know shit about the money. Not soon after that, he was forcing me to suck his funky fishy ass dick. He even made me swallow his nut and I threw up on his ass. Before he could hit me, a car pulled up, and he said, 'I'll be right back you lil nasty bitch.' When he came back, he had a dude with him that I can't seem to get out my head. He looked me straight in my eyes and asked me about the money. I told him I didn't know and he believed me. But what's crazy was he looked just like my dad."

"Did you get a name?" Heads asked pulling his car out of the motel parking lot. "Yes I heard Lo call him Santana I think," I said. Heads slammed on his brakes. "Santana," he yelled. "Yes, that's his name," I said. "Santana is Ray's twin," Heads said looking confused. "What," I yelled. "My father's twin," I thought.

With his hands gripping the steering wheel Heads said "Yes he's your father twin. He never told you much about him because we all knew Santana was in New York serving a life sentence for being caught up in a major drug bust and a few bodies he caught a few years back."

I was looking confused as shit as I yelled "But none of this makes sense to me. If he had a life sentence then why the hell is he out and why is he, looking for money that may or may not even exist that belongs to my dad but claiming that he owes to him? I'm confused as hell now."

A Daughters Rage

"Well right now my only concern is getting you somewhere safe," he said as he started back driving. "If Santana's out then your grandfather, Armando is on his ass. I'm taking you to my house in Upper Marlboro," Heads said driving like a maniac.

The look on his face spoke a thousand words and if I wasn't scared at first I was most definitely scared then. Not only was my uncle whom I'd never met and really didn't know anything about out of jail, but my grandfather one of the most dangerous, ruthless, motherfuckers you could encounter was also in B-more. My father kept me away from Papa Armando because he was very controlling and believed that women were not worthy of being anything but a mother and housewife. Damn Heads must be making money. He had a house in the county. I wonder what else he had. I knew one thing for sure. That motherfucker was fine as wine.

"You can relax shawty because we have about an hour drive," he said. As tired as I was, I was too anxious to sleep. I put my seat back and closed my eyes anyway.

Roni J.

A Daughters Rage

Heads

"What the fuck have I gotten myself into with this lil girl," I thought. For the past couple of years I hadn't heard anything from her and now when shit was changing and getting better for me, she comes into my life with a whole lot of drama. I couldn't lie though she was beautiful. Ray had told me that even though I was 5 years older than her he wanted me to be the man that married his daughter one day. I could never tell her that, she already thought she was the shit and she had made a bad name for herself. I was not feeling that shit at all.

My phone ringing on my lap broke my thoughts. I answered without looking to see who it was. "Hey boo." It was Tracy, my girlfriend. "Yeah, hey baby girl, what's up?" I asked. "You tell me, am I seeing you tonight? You know I miss you and I got a taste for some of that big dick," she said while giggling.

"Shit I forgot about hooking up with her tonight," I thought. "I'm going to have to take a rain check baby. I'm on a run right now and I won't be back in town until morning," I said.

Roni J.

"A run? Where you going Heads, I haven't seen you in 3 days," she sounded so sad and disappointed. "You know I never discuss my bizness with you, so like I said, I'll see you tomorrow." I tried not to sound like I was agitated. Without saying another word, she just hung up.

Tracy was my girl for the last 3 years. She was a good girl. She wasn't like the rest of those hood bitches. She was 5 feet even. Short haircut. Light skin with big bouncy titties and a round ass that drove me crazy. She was a straight A student and lived in a two parent home. She was most definitely my ride or die chick. The only thing about her that I didn't like was that she was too clingy, always wanted to be around me, and know what I was doing. I knew it was only because she worried about me out in those streets. Truth was I did love her and I thought after my mother died I could never love another woman. There was a lot about me that motherfuckers would never understand. I thought I did pretty good when I took my meds but lately I hadn't been taking them because I was on the move stacking my dough so I could get the fuck out of Baltimore. I hated having PTSD. It was my greatest weakness. Ever since my accident, I hadn't been the same. Between hustling,

A Daughters Rage

my son, and my girl I barely took care of myself. I'd have to do better but for the moment, I needed to get Mona to my house and get my ass back to B'more to find out what the fuck was going on. I knew if Armando and Santana were involved it couldn't be good.

Roni J.

A Daughters Rage

University Hospital ICU: Kevin

As I lay there, all I saw was black and I couldn't understand why. I could hear but I couldn't talk. I could feel the tubes in my throat and the machines beeping around me but I couldn't move. "WHERE THE FUCK AM I," I yelled but no one could hear me. "Why the fuck is nobody answering me? What the fuck is going on, and why is it so dark in here?" Then I heard a familiar voice, it was my mother, Carolyn Jones. "Hi Mrs. Jones I'm Doctor Henderson. I'm the doctor who operated on your son. How are you?" he asked.

"Operated? What the fuck is he talking about?" I thought.

"I'm ok under the circumstances but how is my son doing and what are the damages doctor?" my mother asked in a cracked voice to keep from breaking down. "Kevin is lucky to be alive Ma'am. Both his legs, arms, and several ribs are broken. He also has a collapsed lung and suffers from temporal brain damage. He has a long road ahead of him. Right now due to his lung being damaged, he can't breathe on his own so the machine is breathing for him. He's in an induced coma so that we can

133

monitor him but your son is a fighter and made it through surgery with very little complications," the doctor said. Carolyn felt weak and had to grab the doctor for support. "Oh God, my baby," was all she could say and then she got on her knees and started praying.

"So that's why it's so dark. Because my damn eyes are closed. I'm in a fucking coma," I thought. I was in a car accident. I remembered going to see Vanessa at the ward, and leaving upset, but I couldn't remember why. What I did remember was I was driving kind of fast and I heard a crash. Then everything went black and by what the doc just told my mom I was pretty fucked up. I had to focus on getting the fuck out of there. "Why am I so upset? What did Vanessa tell me? Why the fuck can't I remember? I feel like I'm about to lose it! Think Kevin think," I thought.

A Daughters Rage

Jake and Romello

"I'm tired of this motherfucker giving me orders J. I should've never listened to you. This shit is going too far and I didn't take an oath to be a corrupt cop," Romello yelled getting upset.

"You've got to relax baby boy because we're getting paid a nice lump sum for our services," Jake responded with a grin on his face.

"It doesn't matter because I've already put my transfer in. I'm leaving you and Baltimore. I'm tired of this shit and not only that you still haven't told that mooching ass wife of yours and you don't plan on telling her," Romello said putting his head down in disgust.

"You did what? I fucking told you I needed time. You're so fucking selfish! If you want to go, go the fuck on, I don't care no more. This shit is too much for me and I can't take it no more." Jake turned to leave but stopped dead in his tracks when he felt the cold steel of Romello's service weapon on the back of his bald head.

"I don't know who the fuck you think I am

but I'm done being your bitch. You have until the end of the week to tell your wife or I will. Now you can play with my head if you want and I promise you I'll kill you, your wife, and myself. Now there's no need for you turn around or say another word. Just get in your car and pull off," Romello said gritting his teeth.

Jake just stood there startled and in shock at how Romello was acting and that it had come down to that. There was no way in hell that he could tell his wife because if he did, his life would change for the worse and he wasn't prepared for that at all. Jake was known on the streets as "HULK." The hard ass, bald headed, cocky cop that didn't take no shit and would put a bullet through your head before you could blink. He could never be prepared for the embarrassment that came with the city finding out he was gay. He pretended to take heed to what Romello was requesting but secretly he had made his mind up that Romello had to go and he knew exactly how he planned on doing it. He walked to car his car, got in, and pulled off.

A Daughters Rage

Lorenzo

I was laying there in a hospital bed angry, staring at the ceiling, and plotting. "I'm going to kill that nigga! He got me fucked up if he think he's going to lay a finger on me and still live. I don't give a fuck about him being my blood. I killed my mother, my bitch ass father, and forced my sister to suck my dick so that nigga isn't any better," I thought. I began to replay the incident over in over in my head. I walked in on a conversation that clearly I wasn't supposed to hear and then the nigga had the nerve to charge me. Now I had stitches and I was laid up in that funky ass hospital. I sat up on the side of my bed feeling dizzy. "Damn my shit is pounding. Where the fuck are my clothes," I yelled. I was looking around the room and I spotted my jeans thrown across a chair in the corner and my favorite Nike sneakers on the floor beside them, but no shirt. Then I remembered I didn't have one on when I got hurt. Standing up still feeling slightly lightheaded, I walked over to the chair, grabbed my jeans, and put them on. Then my sneakers. I kept on my hospital gown. Peeking outside my room door all I wanted to do was get the fuck out that hospital with no altercations. I stepped out and started walking down the long hallway that led to the elevator. Surprisingly no one stopped me. I got to the elevator and pressed the down button. The door opened, I got on, and left.

"Armando is going to get the same fate as his son did. That nigga didn't want to be a part of my life. He wanted to keep me a secret and I killed his ass for it. Now I'm going to kill Armando as soon as I find out where the money is. Santana is just one of my ponds too," I thought. Then Mona and Kevin. Fuck everybody! The only person who ever loved me was Linda and I killed her for keeping shit from me. I hated a fucking liar. When it was all said and done, I was going to be the last one standing.

"You know this shit ain't going to be that easy right?"

"Who said that?" I asked looking around. I swore I thought I heard a nigga say something. I must've been tripping or I'd hit my head pretty fucking hard. Standing on the curb outside the hospital, I flagged a cab down. Once I was in, I told him where to take me. That motherfucker acted as if he didn't understand English. Fucking Arabs!

A Daughters Rage

Roni J.

A Daughters Rage

Mona

"Wake up sleepy head, we're here," Heads said yelling in my damn ear. I was glad he woke me up. I was having a wild ass dream about Mya. I hadn't talked to her since earlier. I needed to call her and I would as soon as I got in there and rested my damn nerves. We had pulled up to a big brick and wood one story house. The house resembled a cabin. It was huge and beautiful. Two big rose bushes sat on each side along with a long brick path that led up to the front door with a garage attached on the right side. "This place is beautiful. I know he doesn't live here and if he does there has to be a woman living here with him. This place has a woman's touch all over it," I thought. I frowned. Heads sat there staring out the window for a few minutes before saying anything. "What's wrong?" I asked. "So what do you think?" he asked.

"I love it! Whose house is this Heads?"

He laughed. "It's mine, but if you must know I inherited it from my father when he died," he said with a smile.

"Oh ok, well it's nice," I said with a slight

smile. "Thanks. Now let's go in and get you settled. There's plenty of food in here and you can shower and get a good night's sleep with no worries," he said seeming calmer. "This dude really has a personality issue," I thought. "That'll be good. I appreciate it. I really do. Is there a phone I can use? I need to call my best friend and let her know that I'm ok," I said staring.

"Yes the phone is in the kitchen on the wall beside the fridge. Make yourself at home," he said smiling a little.

"Is it me or did this nigga just do a whole 360 turn around?" I thought. I hoped Mya wasn't mad at me. On my way into the kitchen, I couldn't help but to admire the inside of the house. "Damn this place is fly as hell," I thought looking around. In the living room, there was a huge 60-inch flat screen television on the wall. There was huge white leather sofa that was shaped like the letter u, with a diamond shaped glass table in the center. Underneath a big plush white rug was so soft your feet sunk as soon you stepped onto it. Then there was a white and gold fireplace with a huge painting atop it. It was of a handsome man that resembled Heads. "That must be his dad," I thought.

A Daughters Rage

"Hey, is that your dad?" I asked.

"Yes that's my father, Benny Sr.," he said.

"You look just like him."

"Yes I get that a lot," Heads said.

"Benny? So that's his real name," I thought. I made a mental note of that. As I made my way into the kitchen and looked around at the décor of the kitchen I was again mesmerized. Everything was glass and stainless steel. His father must have been a rich motherfucker to have that place laced like that. Damn. I picked up the phone and dialed Mya's number. After the second ring, she answered.

"Hey sister, it's me," I said happily.

"Oh my god Monie! Where the fuck have you been and why did it take you so long to call me back? I was worried sick. Where are you?" Mya asked with a slight attitude.

"Don't worry I'm fine, I'm with Heads right now."

"You're what? Where are you at with him Monie?" Mya asked yelling in the phone. She was completely livid mainly because she didn't like

Heads and she didn't trust him. She didn't trust anybody and I couldn't blame her.

"The less information you know the safer you'll be Mya. I promise you. Now I'm going to talk to him and see if you can come here with me. I don't know exactly where I am but I'm far from the city and I'm safe," I tried to explain so she could relax.

"What do you mean you don't know where you are Monie? Listen to yourself. He can be very dangerous and I'm worried." She began to cry a little.

"Please don't cry. I honestly don't think he's going to do anything to hurt me, he's only trying to help me," I said trying to convince her and myself.

"Ok if you say so. You don't know shit about him and you're assuming because your dad told you to go to him..." Then Mya remembered she had something to tell me. "Monie, it's Kevin," she said.

"Huh? What you mean its Kevin? What about him? I'm pissed off at his lying ass! He told me he was going to get me some food and that he would be right back and he never came. You know what I did to eat Mya? I fucked a trick. That's how I found Heads and..." Mya cut me off before I could finish.

"Kevin was in a real bad car accident with a big rig, you know the front of the big tractor truck," Mya said yelling in the phone.

"Huh? What you just say?" I asked to make sure I had heard her correctly. Everything seemed to go in slow motion. The room began to spin and I started to feel lightheaded. I started shaking my head from side to side in disbelief at what Mya just told me. I also knew Mya would never lie to me about anything, and especially not something so serious.

"MONIE, DID YOU HEAR WHAT THE FUCK I JUST SAID," Mya yelled into the phone again.

I just held the phone pressed hard against my ear. Something didn't feel right. I didn't think Kevin's accident was an accident at all. I felt that it was done on purpose. Simply because he was trying to help me, someone was trying to kill him. What in the fuck was going on in my life? Whoever was after me was on their best bullshit. "Shit just got real," I thought.

Roni J.

"I – I- I'm here Mya. I just don't get this shit. The whole day from the start was fucked up. All of today's events had me fucked up. I don't believe it was an accident at all. I think somebody hit Kevin on purpose to either kill him or send him a message. All because he was trying to help me. Technically, I was supposed to be in the car with him but he convinced me to go to the motel instead. The thought of the hit being intended for me had me sick on the stomach. Look I'm going to be ok," I said trying more to convince my damn self than I was Mya. "I'm about to take a shower and get some sleep. If I don't call you back tonight, I will early in the morning," I said feeling guilty for sending Kevin to get my food.

"Ok sister try getting some rest Monie. Promise you'll call me back in the morning," Mya said not wanting to get off the phone. "Yes bookie I'm going to call you. I promise and I love you," I said. "Love you too. Goodnight," she said.

What I said to Mya made sense but if the hit was intended for me, the situation was far more serious than we thought and shit just got real.

"Judging from your facial expression that phone call didn't go to good," Heads said.

A Daughters Rage

"It didn't. Shit is real. Kevin was in a real bad car accident and is in the hospital fighting for his life. The fucked up part of it all is that I was supposed to be with him but he convinced me to stay at the motel." I started to cry and began to shake. I was a real bitch. "Where the fuck are all these tears coming from?" I thought. "Wherever this money is I hope they find that shit soon and leave me the fuck alone."

Heads felt bad for me mainly because I was dealt a bad hand because of the life my father led. Even though I appeared to be a soldier, I was not built for that life. I was gonna have to learn how to be. Being the daughter of the infamous Ray Ramirez meant shit was going to get worse before it got better.

"Come here Mona," Heads said holding his arms out to give me a hug. At first, I just stood there staring at him confused. Then I walked towards him and accepted his embrace. There was something about the way that he held me that made me feel completely safe and secure in his arms. He smelled so good to me. Heads also felt the strange connection between us and decided to let me go.

Roni J.

"It's going to be ok shorty; Why don't you go get some rest? Goodnight," he said walking away towards his room without saying another word. "Damn what was that about," I thought.

I made my way into the huge bathroom so that I could take a nice hot shower. The shower had a large walk-in marble shower with a chrome shower head and glass sliding door. There was an oversized plush rug in the center of the floor. First, I just stood there in awe at the place. Then I opened the large gold cabinet next to the toilet and saw numerous bars of my favorite Dove soap. "Yes I'm in heaven," I thought. "Yeah he must bring his bitch here because no man uses Dove soap," I laughed to myself. In the other cabinet, I saw towels and wash clothes folded neatly and smelling like Downy fabric softener. I grabbed a bar of soap, wash cloth, and towel, and sat them on the back of the toilet. I got undressed. I pulled the shower door open and turned the water on. Grabbing the washcloth and bar of soap, I stepped into the shower. The water was coming out like a mini waterfall and felt so good against my skin. Lathering my body with soap and gently scrubbing my skin I felt relaxed and comfortable. I began to think about my life once again and the day's events.

A Daughters Rage

None of it made sense to me but I was going to get to the bottom of it even if it killed me. After showering, I went into the guest bedroom, climbed into the huge king sized bed completely naked, and went to sleep.

Roni J.

A Daughters Rage

Jake

I sat in my car replaying the conversation I had with Romello over and over in my mind and the whole ordeal made me angrier by the minute. I couldn't help but think back to the day I met him. It was August 19, 2010, almost 2 years ago. Lieutenant Scott introduced the new officer and I knew immediately that he was going to be a handful. I thought I was ready but what I didn't know was that Romello had secrets and was just as dangerous, if not more dangerous, than myself. However, I would soon find out.

I pulled up to my home preparing to face my wife. Stepping out of my car something felt strange and I became worried. My wife's car wasn't parked out front. Maybe she had gotten a ride home but that wasn't normal. I immediately dialed my wife's cell phone but to no avail. I called her office and was told that Shelly had left over an hour ago. "I know this motherfucker has something to do with this shit!" Romello was the first person who popped in my mind because he'd been making threats. That was the last straw for me. That nigga had to go and he had to go that night. If he laid a

Roni J.

finger on my wife or if a hair was out of place I was going to put a hole in his fucking head. I hopped back in my car, pulled out of my driveway, and headed to Romello's house with murder on my mind.

I was so angry that I wasn't paying attention to the black Escalade truck parked directly across the street from my house watching me, and now following me. I had one thing on my mind and that was putting my murder game down. I picked up my phone to make a call that I should have been made, but with all that had been going on I forgot. "Hey man how you holding up?" I asked. I finally noticed the truck tailing me in the rear view but couldn't make out the driver.

"I'm making it. Why has it taken you so long to call and how is she?" the person on the other end asked. "Right now I don't know where she is, but I promise on my life I'm going to find her man. It's just that I have a lot going on in my own life right now," I tried to explain.

"I don't give a fuck about you or your life. I could fuck your whole world up if I wanted to. Now you've got 24 hours to call me back. When you do you better know where the fuck she is or

A Daughters Rage

you can prepare your sweet momma to bury her son," the caller yelled in my ear. Before I could respond, the line went dead.

It seemed as if everybody thought I was some kind of bitch or something. It was time to start showing those niggas why I had the name "HULK." I banged my fist on the steering wheel so hard that I almost lost control of my car. I was so angry I thought I needed a drink. A drink was what I am going to get, but something I definitely didn't need. I turned and made a right on to Highland Ave and I noticed the truck was still behind me. I made another right onto East St and I noticed whoever it was wasn't behind me anymore so I kept going. Those niggas thought I was dumb! They were going to keep testing me and shit was going to get real ugly.

Roni J.

A Daughters Rage

Mona

"Damn I slept so good," I said stretching my arms and legs out while still lying in the bed. I knew one thing for sure. I was starving. I grabbed the oversized tee shirt he gave me to sleep in and put it on. "Let me go in here and see what he has in this kitchen that I can whip up real fast," After washing my face and brushing my teeth, I made my way into the kitchen. To my surprise, there was plenty of food. "Ok Heads I hear that shit," I thought smiling to myself. I decided to make some bacon, cheese eggs, and grits with lots of butter. Damn I was hungry. There had to be a radio around there. Looking around I noticed a stereo built in the wall near the stove. That was some fly shit. I loved music and I loved to sing. Fumbling through the stations trying to see what was on the radio I heard Trey Songz's "Be Where You Are." That was my shit. I started to sing along. "When she hit the club heads turn," I sang while I gathered what I was going to need for my breakfast. I wondered if I should see if Heads wanted something to eat. I walked towards his room but before I decided to knock, I heard him on the phone. I decided to ear hustle. "I fell asleep baby girl, why all the questions? I'll be in town in about an hour," he said to whoever was on the phone. Baby girl? I wondered who that was. Maybe it was his girlfriend. Fuck it, that bitch could fix him something to eat. Ugh! Rolling my eyes, I turned to walk away but I made a mistake and hit the door and it opened a little. "Shit, I hope he didn't see me," I thought. I tip toed back towards the kitchen. "Open the door," he said. Shit, he did see me. That shit was embarrassing. I turned around and said, "I just came to ask if you wanted something to eat?"

"Yeah what you fixing?" he asked. "Bacon, eggs, and grits," I said with a fake smile. "Cool," he said. "Aye I was wondering if you could pick Mya up and bring her out here with me please?" I asked. "I'm not into to many people knowing where my house at ma so I hope I won't regret this, but aright shawty. I got you," he said smiling and I noticed he had a dimple. "THANK YOU," I yelled excitedly. I got really excited. "Once I cook for this nigga he's going to be putty in my hands," I thought. "Yo call shawty and tell her be ready around 4," he said. "Aight," was all I said. After smashing the meal I cooked him, Heads got dressed and left. I got on the phone trying to find out what hospital Kevin was in. After calling three different ones, I found him at University. They wouldn't give me much over the phone, only that he was in the shock/trauma ICU, which meant he was really bad off. "Oh my God. Lord please let him be ok. I didn't mean for any of this to happen to him. What the fuck is going on?" I yelled. Besides Mya, I really didn't trust anybody but Kevin. I was kind of iffy about Heads for now but I thought I needed to call my grandmother.

Roni J.

A Daughters Rage

Armando's Warehouse

The doc called and said Lo left the hospital. "If he thinks that we tried to hurt him he's going to come for us and that'll be the worst mistake he will ever make," Armando said. Santana began rubbing his hands together as he felt his blood pressure rising "I'm out on parole. I can't be doing shit to bring attention to myself so I hope the lil nigga don't come for me because I will kill his young ass, nephew or not," he yelled getting angrier. "Let me go see what the fuck this bitch doing," he said walking off. Armando got on the phone.

"This shit is more of a headache than I thought. Lo is a problem. Sandy swears she doesn't know where the money is, Mona is missing, and Kevin is fighting for his life. Do you really feel that this shit is worth it?" Armando asked the man that was on the other end of the call. "Yes I do. There's a reason for it all and in due time you will see old man. Now find her!" The phone went dead. Armando was so angry he threw the phone across the warehouse almost hitting the flat screen. He couldn't believe that he had lost power like that and that he was taking orders from who he was

Roni J.

taking them from. Shit was about to get real ugly. He called Jake but got no answer so he called Romello and got his voicemail. "Shit," he yelled. "I think I'm gonna have to kill one of those fags to find out where the fuck my granddaughter is. Before it's all said and done it's going to be a blood bath and I'll be the reason they call it Body-more Murda-land," he thought.

A Daughters Rage

Jake

I pulled up to Romello's house gun in hand. Looking around I realized how uppity that nigga was when I noticed a white elderly man jogging down the street. "Ha!" I laughed to myself shaking my head. I knew he was there because his truck was parked out front. I got out; walked up to the house, and using my key I let myself in. It was very dark and the atmosphere seemed off. "Aye Mello I know you in here my nigga," I yelled out. I heard footsteps above my head so I moved slowly throughout the house moving towards the stairs. Before I could move any further I heard Mello say, "One move and I'll blow your fucking head off. You must've thought I was playing with you nigga. Your wife is upstairs and she knows everything. She's just waiting for you to confirm it so we can get on with our lives baby," he said looking crazed. "I thought I told you to stay the fuck away from my wife nigga," I yelled. I turned and took off up the steps yelling out to my wife.

"Shelly! Shelly! Where are you baby?" She didn't answer so I ran to every room until I get to his bedroom. Oh, my God, that motherfucker was crazy. That sick bitch had my wife tied up to a chair with a rag in her mouth. "Baby I'm here now. You're going to be ok." Romello came in the room. "Now why are you making promises you can't keep J? I told you I was going to kill you, her, and me but I have a lot to live for my love so I decided that her time was up. Now I knew you would do this so you see that red dot on her head? All I have to do is push the call button and it's over." He laughed.

"You really are a crazy motherfucker but I'm crazier. Now I'm going give you one more chance to let my wife go or you die right here, right now," I yelled. However, it was too late. He hit the button and his friend next door took the shot. The window came crashing down ending my wife's life. It happened so fast. I couldn't do shit but hold my wife. Her blood splattered all over my face and hands. Romello took off leaving me there with my dead wife. "No," I yelled. "Shelly baby wake up! Shells please baby." I knew she was gone but I just couldn't let her go. I sat there and waited for the police. Within minutes, the Baltimore Police Department and the crime lab had the house swarmed and I was under arrest for murdering my wife. "Freeze Officer Robinson! Put your fucking hands on your head now," Ratcliff yelled. He couldn't stand my ass and it was just my luck that his KKK ass would be the arresting officer. I was about to try and explain but I felt defeated so I let it go for now. I figured I wouldn't be put in general population because I was a cop. They would put me in lock up or at least I was hoping they would, but at that point, I didn't even give a fuck. I was devastated that my wife was gone. I wouldn't be locked up long because I didn't kill my wife and the evidence would prove that. If I did get put in lock up that would be my down time because I was going to kill Mello and everybody else who had something to do with the murder of my wife. Containing me would be best for everybody at that point. When they let me out, I was going on a murder trip. Those niggas weren't ready!

Roni J.

A Daughters Rage

Mona

"Hey Mya he said be ready by 4. He's picking you up."

"Ok sister but I'm still unsure about him. His ass is crazy and I'm worried he may snap," Mya said with her paranoid ass.

"He wants us to think he's crazy but nobody's crazier than me. I'm Ray and Sandy Ramirez's child. I was born crazy. Now stop worrying. We have to plan our shit right and precise. I need your mind clear of the bullshit," I said laughing.

"Ok let me get my shit. I'll call you back. I love you," Mya said before she hung up.

I had to find out where they were holding Sandy's dirty ass. I hoped they hadn't killed her yet because I wanted to so bad. I trusted my gut that the bitch knew what happened to my daddy. The connection I had with him I believed would help me get to the bottom of that shit. I was thinking I should call Grandma Selma. I hadn't spoken to her in months and I knew she was worried. I picked up

Roni J.

the phone to dial and a feeling of anxiety washed over me. Damn! What the fuck was wrong with me? My hand was shaking yet again. I had to get it together. With the phone pushed to my ear and my leg shaking, I wondered if Grandma would sense that something was wrong. "Hola," my grandmother answered. I smiled as my grandmother said hello in Spanish. "Hola Abuela," I said remembering that Abuela means grandmother in Spanish. I loved to hear my grandma's voice. She was a full-blooded Puerto Rican and spoke mostly Spanish. "Si Mona. Is that you baby," she asked. "Si Abuela it's me," I responded speaking in Spanish and English. "I've missed you. How are you?" I asked. My eyes began to water because I knew I wouldn't have gone through what I had if I would have gone with my grandmother after Daddy died. However, Sandy's evil ass wouldn't allow it. "I'm much better now that you called. I've been worried about you baby," she said with uncertainty in her voice. "I'm not going to tell you I'm ok Grandma because I'm not. Things are really crazy around here. I miss my dad so much it makes me sick. But I did want to call you and see if you were ok," I said trying to reassure her that I'd be ok. "Baby you're just a child. You shouldn't have to carry the burdens of adults. Just say the word and I'll book a flight for you to come to Miami," she said. I almost flipped off the chair. I wanted to go so badly but I couldn't leave then. "There's too much shit going on," I thought. "Grandmother allow me to get a few things in order and I promise you I'll call you in a week ok," I said. "Si Mona I'm going to hold you to that. Adios."

"Ok Adios Abuela. Te amo," I said in Spanish. "Te amo," she said before hanging up. It felt so good to hear someone tell me that they loved me.

Roni J.

A Daughters Rage

Carolyn Jones's House

Ring! Ring! Ring! "Lord, what did I do with that phone," Carolyn thought before spotting it on the sofa. "Hello Jones residence," Carolyn answered.

"Hi Mrs. Jones, this is nurse Joan Kelly calling from Sheppard Pratt mental facility. I'm calling you to inform you that, I'm sorry Ma'am, there's no easy way to tell you this, but Vanessa Brown committed suicide last night. When the orderlies conducted the morning count, she was found in her bathroom on the floor again. I am so sorry." Joan was a little shaken up herself; she had grown to love Vanessa. She was holding back her tears.

"What," Carolyn yelled. "When? How did this happen," she demanded. "Ma'am I understand you're upset, but trust me, we didn't know that Mrs. Brown had stolen the pair of scissors she used to cut her wrist. We found her early this morning. The other reason I called you for is she left a letter for your son Kevin and I wanted to let Mr. Jones know that. So if you can have him give me a call please I'd appreciate it," she said.

"Well that won't be possible because my son is in a coma. He was in a bad car accident," Carolyn said breaking down. Joan couldn't believe what Carolyn had just told her, mainly because she had seen Kevin the day before when he went to the facility to see Vanessa. Joan held the phone for a few minutes shaking her head and wiping a tear that was about to fall. She couldn't believe what was happening within that family. All she could do was tell Carolyn how sorry she was which she knew wouldn't change anything. "Ok Mrs. Jones and again I'm sorry about everything. If you need anything can you please call me back on my private number?" Joan said in a sad tone. "That's really nice of you sweetie but all I need for you to do is pray for my entire family. Thank you." Before Joan could reply, Carolyn had hung up. She knew that Kevin would be hurt about Vanessa dying because he loved her. She was his birth mother. However, Carolyn's focus was her son and getting him back to health was her main priority.

A Daughters Rage

Sandy

Santana came walking in on me. What the fuck did he want? Lo had already raped and beat the fuck out of me. It was a task just to keep breathing. "Just kill my ass already," I thought. "Damn girl Lo fucked you up good," he said with a grin looking at me. I didn't say shit. I just continued to stare. I figured if I give his ass the silent treatment he would leave me the fuck alone. Santana had an evil smirk on his face as he said "I'm past tired of playing this game with you bitch. I know you know where the money is just like I know you had my brother set up. Now I bet you're trying to figure out how I know but you'll find that out in due time. I tried to warn Ray about your needy ass but he wouldn't listen," he said looking at me with a raised eyebrow. My eyes were bulging out. "How do he know that I had Ray set up," I thought.

"I don't know what you're talking about," I said looking away. "Don't play with me bitch! You're pissing me off," Santana said yelling in my face. "I really don't know anything about the money Santana. I swear to you I don't," I said while looking him straight in the eye. He was staring down at me. I believed he knew I was telling the truth. He turned and walked away. Once again, my life was spared. I noticed the only time it got really cold in that bitch was when they closed the door. Looking around I thought I was in some sort of freezer. I was so cold that my teeth were chattering and my lips were trembling. "What the fuck are those crazy fools planing to do to my ass next," I wondered.

A Daughters Rage

Lorenzo

As angry as I was, I was chilling lying across Tonya's bed. Tonya thought she was cute. She was a hoe ass bitch but it didn't matter because I was not trying to wife the hoe. She could cook, I could eat, we fucked there, and nobody knew. I didn't expect motherfuckers to know I was there. I knew that those bitch ass niggas thought I was still in the hospital.

"You most definitely can't sleep on those niggas my nigga."

I jumped up looking around to see who the fuck said that but I knew I was alone in Tonya's house. That wasn't the first time I thought I heard a nigga talking to me. I must've been cracking the fuck up. I lay back down flat on my back staring at the ceiling. I needed to find that nigga Light Skin Mac. He was my lil brother's father and I heard he was coming for me. Niggas just keep getting themselves put on my knock off list. I thought back to Mona sucking my dick. I really was a dirty ass nigga but it was justified or was it? I hated that lil bitch. If it wasn't for her, my father wouldn't be

Roni J.

dead. She was born and he forgot about my ass. My reason for wanting her dead was plain and simple. She shouldn't have been born. The way I saw it, I didn't have shit to lose. My momma was gone and my bitch ass deadbeat father was gone. Both at my hands so what the fuck was the point. I had to finish what I started. Counting on my fingers, I added up the motherfuckers who had got to go. Mona, Kevin, Sandy, Mac, Armando, and Santana. That city would never be prepared for the bloodshed that was about to hit those streets. If niggas didn't know me, they soon would. My fucking name was Black!

A Daughters Rage

Baltimore City Police Department

As I sat there handcuffed and shackled like the criminal that I truly am, I couldn't help but to find irony in that shit. I thought of all the fucked up shit I had done to people and all the laws I had broken. I was supposed to catch the bad guys but I spent more time being one himself. I smiled. "I don't know how this shit is going to play out but I have some lil niggas on my team that are treacherous, straight killers, and when I get my phone call I will make my move," I thought.

"So Jake you little prick, I told you I would get your black ass and I did," Officer Ratcliff chanted.

I just smiled which pissed Ratcliff off. The two of us had been going after one another for almost a year. Ratcliff was a racist standing at 6 feet tall, skinny with big feet, blonde dirty hair, and his teeth were yellow and brown stained from drinking too much coffee and smoking.

"Oh you can laugh all you want. I got your black ass now and once you get behind them walls, my boys are going to make you their bitch. I bet

Roni J.

you would like that wouldn't you," Ratcliff whispered while smiling and showing his nasty ass teeth. That statement caught me off guard and I almost flipped out. I started shaking and my eyes became red as fire. No one knew about my sexuality or did they? Ratcliff continued smiling before walking off. He knew he had hit a nerve with Jake and that's exactly what he wanted to do.

A Daughters Rage

Heads

As I was driving down 95, I thought about shorty back at my house. She was beautiful and her body was banging, but I couldn't go there. I had a girl and I was happy. She did cook me breakfast though which I couldn't remember Tracey ever doing, but I had to stay focused on helping shorty get out of whatever situation she was in. I promised Ray that I would and I was a man of my word. I thought back to something I heard my favorite rapper Tupac Shakur say. "All I'm trying do is survive and make good out of the dirty, nasty, unbelievable lifestyle they gave me." That's what I told myself every day. I wanted a better life for my son and myself and the only way I saw it happening was getting the fuck out of that city.

Listening to Tupac blasting through my car speakers and talking to myself, I didn't realize I was almost to my destination. Pulling up on the block I spotted this lil shorty named Kimberly. She knew how to get to me dressing the way she dressed. I laughed because every lil hood chick had been coming for me ever since they found out Tracey was wifey. Kimberly wasn't shit though;

most of my niggas had hit that pussy. She probably hadn't got a bottom in that ass. I noticed my lil dude Shawn walking towards my car. He was only 15 but he was smart and he was out here trying to get it, looking out for his mama. I could appreciate a lil nigga trying to get out of the hood. "Aye Shawn, what's up my dude," I said. Shawn started smiling showing his dimples like he always did. "Aye big homey! Ain't shit. Trying to get this money, you know how I do. I saw you when you pulled up so I had to come holler at you feel me?" Shawn asked dapping me. "Yeah I feel you," I said. "I got a few moves to make but I'll hit you later G." Shawn dapped me again before jogging back across the street.

As soon as I stepped out of my car crack head ass Melba came walking up on me begging, and I hated that shit. "Look Melba take this $20 and get the fuck on," I yelled. I knew she was going to get high but right then, I didn't give a fuck. She snatched it and ran off. All I could do was shake my head. I walked over to a crew of young niggas shooting dice. I said a few words and hopped back in my car pulling off en route to pick lil shorty, grateful she was around the corner. I honked my horn. She came out looking nervous and it threw me off. I think I saw her lil ass next door to my cousin Tammy's, but I wasn't sure. "All those lil bitches look alike," I thought. I reached over opening the passenger door for her to get in and she looked unsure. I didn't want to scare her but I really didn't have time for that shit. "Mona asked me to pick you up but if you don't want to go I can take my ass on. I got shit to do," I said trying not to sound too aggressive. She walked up to the car and got in without saying a word so I didn't say shit else. She closed the door and I pulled off. "Look I have to make a quick stop then I'm going to take you to Mona," I said while driving. All she did was nod her head. And they had a nerve to call me crazy. "Tuh," I thought.

Roni J.

A Daughters Rage

Mona

Seriously, what the fuck was taking that nigga so long. I was feeling like I was about to have an anxiety attack! I had so many thoughts running through my mind. I was wondering if Mya would submit to my plans or if her paranoid ass would crumble under pressure. I was built for that shit. She wasn't. I was going to ask Heads if he'd teach me how to shoot. I hadn't been to the range since my father took me. If not, I'd teach my damn self. Right at that moment, all I had was murder and pain on my mind. With all the shit that was happening I was 100% sure Sandy's evil ass had my father killed. I just needed the proof and when that happened, I was going to lose it on that hoe. Just as I was getting worked up, I heard a car pull up. I knew it was Heads and Mya because he said no one else knew where he lived. Or did he say he didn't want people knowing? I didn't know. Either way I was about to find out. I ran to the door, swung it open, and I saw Mya smiling but Heads looked angry as shit. I shrugged. "Oh well," I thought. Mya got out of the car first throwing her backpack over her shoulder with a relieved look on her face. Once she reached the door, Heads started the car back up, stuck his head out the window, and said, "Get in the house," before he pulled off and left. "Dude is crazy," Mya said laughing. "Yeah he's got issues, but he's not crazy," I said. "Now it's time for me to go over my plan with Mya. I'll get back to him later," I thought. Walking in the house, I noticed Mya looking around. "This place is fly," she said. "Yeah it is," I said. "You hungry?" I asked. "Not hungry but thirsty," she said. "Ok we have water, apple juice, and orange juice."

"Water," Mya said.

"Ok we need to talk sister. We have plans to make and I need you fully on board, you feel me," I said tossing Mya her bottled water. She looked at me smiling and said, "Ok let's get it."

"That's what the fuck I'm talking about," I yelled pumped up.

A Daughters Rage

Kevin

I laid there still in a coma in disbelief at what I heard the doctor say to my adoptive mother. I still couldn't remember everything, but bits and pieces were coming back to me slowly. I concentrated only on the conversation that I had with Vanessa, but the only thing I remembered was her telling me something about Mona being my sister. Everything else was a blur. "Come on Kev, think dammit," I thought. I could hear the nurses in my room as they had been in and out ever since I'd been there. There was a familiar voice that I heard then and it was the chick from the reception desk at the mental hospital where Vanessa was. "What's she doing here," I wondered. Maybe Ness had found out about the accident and sent her to check on me. Then I heard her say, "Hi my name is Joan, and I'm here just to see how Mr. Jones is doing." "I'm sorry Miss, are you family?" the nurse asked. "No I'm not. I work at the hospital where his mom was housed," Joan replied. "Oh well. I'm sorry Miss Joan but if you're not family then you can't be in here," the nurse told Joan. "Oh ok. I didn't mean to intrude. I was just checking on him. I'll go now," she said walking out of the room.

Roni J.

"These people are something else around here. They just come walking up in these patients rooms demanding info. They really need to get better security on these ICU floors," one nurse said to the other nurse. "Yes I agree. I heard them say Mr. Jones wasn't in an accident at all but that someone attempted to kill him. I don't know if it's true though." Then they both left me alone in the room with my thoughts. What the fuck they mean somebody tried to kill me and what did Joan mean when she said the mental facility where my mother was housed? Shouldn't she be saying is housed? What the fuck is going on? I was so confused and upset that I couldn't do shit. I was helpless, and had no way of telling them that I was awake, and had heard everything.

A Daughters Rage

Romello

I was on the run now yet again. I knew that the truth was going to come out about everything so I gathered a few clothes, my lock box, and hit the interstate headed down south. I planned to go to Mexico and start a new life. I hoped that would be my last time running. I knew that Ratcliff was going to try to prolong the investigation as long as possible. Not because he hated Jake so much, but that he loved him that much. I had done this shit before and now I was starting over yet again. This time as Tony Hamilton. The lock box that I had consisted of my life's biggest secrets, fake ID's and driver's licenses, passports, fake business cards, and stacks of 100 dollar bills that totaled 100,000 dollars. I had the money from a bank robbery up in New York right before I came to Baltimore. I also had a mini .22-Magnum revolver that was my favorite. It was small and compact, easy to hide, and it held a body count of at least 25. I was a natural born killer and common criminal. What I didn't know was that Jake was also a crazy motherfucker and I had met my match. I would never admit it but I was a little scared of Jake. "I know that nigga's going to come looking for me,

Roni J.

but he won't find me," I said laughing to himself while speeding down the highway.

A Daughters Rage

Sandy

I lay on the cold concrete floor of Armando's warehouse going in and out of consciousness; I was bleeding from almost every hole on my body. My right eye was closed shut from Lo punching me in it. I could barely see and the way my body was positioned I was lying on my left side with little vision in my left eye.

With what little vision I did have, I could see a shadow of some sort but couldn't make out what it was. It looked like a person and that's exactly what it was. It was Ray, I was sure of it that time. "Oh my God Ray! Is that really you baby? Did you really come for me? I'm so sorry baby. I didn't mean for them to hurt you. I just wanted to teach you a lesson I swear," I mumbled and got no response. The shadow walked in my direction and stopped directly in front of me looking down. Looking up I was sure it was Ray but before I could open my mouth and say anything, he lifted up his right foot and brought it down on the side of my face so hard my head bounced off the concrete like a ball. The hit shattered my right jawbone knocking me out. "Get this bitch up," the unknown man said

Roni J.

to the two men he brought with him. "Put her ass in the chest and have her loaded up. I'll meet y'all at the port in an hour." The two men did what they were told. The unknown man got on the phone and made a call. "Yes I'm here now but I won't be for long. I'm headed out. Meet me down at the port in an hour. I have one more move to make." Then he hung up.

A Daughters Rage

Mona

"Ok so what's the plan?" Mya asked while smashing on the homemade BLT that I just made for her. "First we need to play the fifty with Lo and make him think we're on his team. That way we can find out if he knows anything about Kevin's accident or if he did the shit himself. He thinks I was scared of his ass, which I am not. I was just a little leery, but fuck all of that. I have to act like I like that nigga to get what the fuck I want," I said with a smirk.

"Yeah but will that work Mona? I mean the nigga may be crazy but he's smart as hell. He got away with murdering his mother and brother," Mya said with a dumb look on her face. She was really blowing me with that bullshit. Sometimes she acted like a bird. "Ugh," I thought as I rolled my eyes.

"We are going to have to get back to the city or somehow get the word out to Lo that I'm looking for his ass, or maybe even lure him out here. Maybe if I posted a status on my Facebook page that would spread the word faster," I said laughing.

Roni J.

"Monie have you lost your damn mind? One crazy nigga is enough! I know you're not going to bring Lo out here to his house! You're trying to get us both killed out this bitch," Mya yelled. Then her phone rang. She took it out of her bag, looked at it, looked up at me, and then pressed the ignore button. She looked at me smiling and said, "Niggas is annoying."

Of all the years I'd known Mya she'd never been a good liar. I could remember when we were in first grade and she stole a piece of candy from our teacher Mrs. Lemon's candy jar. The whole class had to stay in during recess because no one would admit it that they had stolen the candy. Mya sat directly behind me with the dumbest look on her face and a half smile that immediately gave away that she was the one who stole the candy. Right then, she had that same dumb ass look. "What niggas Mya?" I asked. "I didn't know you were talking to anybody," I said.

"There's some things I don't tell you Monie," she said with slight attitude in her voice. I caught that shit but I decided to ignore it. Something was most definitely up with her and I didn't like it. "Oh ok. Anyway, we need to figure out a way to set Lo up. When Heads gets back I'm going to let him know what I plan to do, so are you down or not?" I asked.

"I still don't think it's a good idea but if you want me to then yeah, I'm down," she said. It was taking all my strength not to check that bitch who I thought was my best friend. "Since when do you do things that I want you to do Mya? That's not how we operate so why start now? I won't be mad. It's either yes or no," I yelled and I had her fucking attention. "Yes Monie I'm down," she said in a sad tone. I didn't give a fuck about that. She acting real shady right now. Tuh! "Now that's what I like to hear," I said walking off.

Mya sat there fuming. "That bitch gets on my nerve sometimes I swear," she thought looking in the direction of Monie. "Hold up Monie what are you about to do," Mya yelled out trying to drown out her phone ringing again. "Shit! What the fuck do he want? I hope she didn't hear my phone ringing," Mya thought. While Monie was in the bathroom Mya took the opportunity to send a text to the caller that said, "Stop calling me I'll hit you back when I can. Damn! Give me a little time," and she ended it with a smiley face.

Roni J.

A Daughters Rage

Lorenzo

That shit was pissing me off. You couldn't send a bitch to do a real nigga's job! All I wanted was a burrito bowl from Chipotle and a bag of loud. I'd been in that damn house all day feeling as if I was about to lose my fucking mind. I swore I kept hearing shit but I knew I was there by myself. That's how I knew I had to get the fuck out of there.

"Nigga you ain't hearing shit. You want to believe you are, to make yourself feel better and justified ahaaa haaaaa," there went the voice again.

"Aye my nigga come out and show your fucking face! Don't hide bitch! Come out," I yelled beating on my chest.

"I'll come out when my opportunity presents itself," the voice said.

"Yo, I'm fucking tripping," I thought. I got up from the sofa. Walking through the house, I opened doors looking in all the rooms yelling. "When I find your bitch ass, its goodnight whore. You fucking with the wrong nigga, G!" As soon as I made my way back in the front room, Tonya

Roni J.

walked in the front door and I lost it. "Bitch you like fucking with me huh," I yelled in her face pushing her against the wall and grabbing her by her throat.

Tonya was terrified. She didn't know what the fuck I was talking about. My hand was around her throat so tight her eyes were bugged out and her face was turning red. "You got some niggas up in this bitch?" I asked realizing I had my hand around her throat and she couldn't answer. I loosened my grasp and let her go. She slid down the wall coughing and gasping for air. "Get your shit together and get the fuck out my house Lo I can't do this shit no more. I don't know what niggas you talking about. It's been just you and me here all week," Tonya said crying and struggling to breathe. I just stood there looking down at her. A part of me wanted to believe her and a part of me knew I couldn't because I was sure that some niggas were in that house and that they had left right before she came home as they always did. "Yeah aight bitch I'll leave, but I will be back. So you can tell those bitch ass niggas that you so call have babysitting me to get ready," I yelled walking out the door and slamming it.

A Daughters Rage

Tonya

I just sat there crying because I had grown to love Lo and knew that he needed mental help. The last thing I needed to do was be pregnant by him. "Now is not the time to tell him but I promise we're going to get Daddy the help that he needs," she said while rubbing her stomach. I had found out earlier that day that I was 7 weeks pregnant. I reached in the bag that was over my shoulder, grabbed my cell phone, and called my cousin Twan.

Roni J.

A Daughters Rage

Heads

Driving down 95 headed back to my house in Upper Marlboro I had my driver's seat laid back, window down, enjoying the late night breeze listening to my favorite rapper Tupac as usual. I had done a little investigation while I was moving about the city. I had found out exactly who Lo was and knowing how the nigga got down, it was going to make things a lot harder than I anticipated. I had a run in with Lo last summer at a cookout that Tracey's family had thrown. He had come with Tonya; Tracey's cousin and another neighborhood hoe. Shaking my head I was happy Tracey wasn't that type of chick. Lo had sat across from me at the picnic table grilling me hard as if he had beef or something. I was the type of nigga that got real worked up so I kept my cool and simply asked Lo, "My nigga I couldn't help but notice you staring at me. Do you have a problem?"

"I'm not your nigga and naw I don't have a problem, but you do," Lo said and I laughed and asked "Oh yeah and what's that?" Lo responded by saying, "Me," and got up and walked away from the table. I thought nothing of it until everybody

Roni J.

was leaving and Lo bumped into me pushing me to the side. We got into a brief scuffle but nothing became of it. I had memory issues due to my brain injury so I had totally forgotten about Lo after the cookout but had been hearing Lo's name in the street a lot lately prior to the situation with Mona. However, the situation that peaked my interest was that I heard Lo set his own house on fire killing his mother and baby brother. "This nigga is going to be a bigger problem if I don't nip this shit in the bud or dead this nigga," I thought. Time had flown by and I just realized I was pulling up to my house. Bringing my car to a stop in front of my garage, I grabbed my garage door opener from my glove compartment and pressed the green button to open. I pulled inside shutting off my car engine and I used the same garage opener to close the door. I stayed in the car thinking about how I was going to break shit down to Mona about how things had to be done on my terms in order for the shit to work. Mona must've been up waiting for me because when I looked up at the door inside that led to the kitchen she was standing there looking directly at me. "Damn! She is so beautiful," I thought. She came out closing the door lightly. Walking around to the passenger side she got in and turned to me with the most serious face she

A Daughters Rage

could muster and simply said, "We need to talk."

Roni J.

A Daughters Rage

Armando's Warehouse

I wasn't known for slipping up because and I never had up until then. Not only was I taking orders from a motherfucker who used to take them from me but now I couldn't find Sandy and I was completely livid. I got on the phone and called Santana. "Where the fuck is she," I yelled in the phone while pacing. "What the fuck you talking about Pops? Where the fuck is who?" Santana yelled back equally. "Look nigga I don't have time for this shit where the fuck is Sandy? You said you were going to talk to the bitch and now she's gone," I said still yelling with spit flying out of my mouth.

"Seriously you need to calm the fuck down. That's first, and second, that bitch was too fucked up and could barely move. On the edge of death, if you ask me so there isn't no way she left on her own. The only other person who would know where she is would be Lo," Santana said.

"Now why the fuck would Lo take her? What good is she to him?" I asked much calmer than before.

"Look I'm on my way hold tight," Santana

Roni J.

said hanging up the phone. I was pacing so hard and I was beginning to make myself dizzy. I was completely baffled. Why would Lo take Sandy and how could he get her out of there without me knowing?

A Daughters Rage

Sandy

I was tied up and stuffed in a chest about 40 inches wide and 1 foot deep and I was five foot seven. I couldn't move any of my limbs but managed to look around just a little. I had been in and out of it for quite some time now and the right side of my face was hanging bloody with broken bones. Pain was all I felt. My body was 90% numb and the bleeding never stopped. The smell inside the chest was foul due to my blood, vomit, and urine. I could only move my pinky finger on my left hand, which I gently wiggled a little from time to time.

"This shit is crazy. I know I've been fucked up so bad and I'm barely alive, but I know my damn eyes weren't playing tricks on me this time. I may have thought Armando was him the first time and I was wrong, but this time I am certain," I thought. Then I heard voices that were too close for comfort. "Let's just drop this bitch in the ocean and get down to bizness. I am not a babysitter," an unknown voice said. "Naw that's not the plan. We have to do this shit the right way," another male voice responded. Before the first guy could say anything, someone else came in the room and that time it was a female. "I can hear the two of you bickering like bitches and you need to cut the shit. Now as much as I would like to drop this bitch in the ocean like the shark she is, I can't. Now y'all know how strategic he is and he does nothing that isn't planned out from A to Z. Dropping her in the ocean isn't an option right now," the female said with a giggle. The second male spoke again and that time I remembered hearing his voice before. It was Light Skin Mac. Linda's other baby father. Now I really was confused. "What the fuck is really going on," I thought before passing out again.

A Daughters Rage

The Conversation

I sat there with my hands clasped together. Staring straight ahead at nothing in particular as I listened to Mona. "So I was thinking I play a little mind game with..." I cut her off mid-sentence. "No mind games. I'm not into that kind of shit," I said angrily but without raising my voice.

She continued. "I plan to convince Lo that I'm on his team so he'll open up and maybe tell me what the fuck he's up to."

All I could do was shake my head "That won't work you have to understand the type of nigga you dealing with. A nigga like Lo is already fucked up in the head so trying to run a mind game on him won't work. The nigga is already crazy and paranoid as shit. You'll be playing Russian Roulette with your life fucking with that nigga," I explained still looking straight ahead.

"Oh. Even though I didn't look at it that way I still feel I can pull it off, and I need you to do something else for me," she said.

"And what's that?" I asked turning my head

and looking at her.

"I want you teach me how to shoot," she said putting her tiny right hand on top of my clasped hands. "I haven't been since my dad took me and I need a refresher course."

I looked her directly in her eye and said, "I thought you would never ask."

Mona smiled. "This nigga isn't crazy. He has a soft spot for me and I can feel it," she thought. "And there's something else that's bothering me even though it may be nothing. I still think it needs to be addressed though," she said. I nodded my head letting her know she could continue. "Mya had been acting a little strange since she got here and the shit was killing my vibe. She was paranoid and being extra secretive. For as long as I can remember, we shared everything and to my knowledge, she's not even fucking. Now her phone's jumping off and she's claiming its niggas that are annoying. Tuh," Mona said with an attitude.

"Well for starters if she's your best friend then you would know these things and what you need to do if you must know who's calling her phone is ask her. And if she doesn't tell you then maybe you need to get her phone and see who it is yourself," I said being sarcastic. "Now I'm going to talk to my girl and see if she can find out from her cousin where Lo is and get word back to him that you're looking for him. That will lure him out and we'll be on his ass like flies on shit. Once she get back to me I'll let you know and we can take it from there." I was getting ready to step out of the car but Mona grabbed my arm. I looked at her like she had lost her mind but when I saw that she was smiling I relaxed.

"I just wanted to say thank you and ask if maybe you could take me to my father's grave site when you get the chance?"

"Yeah I think I can do that," I said with a half-smile. Though it had only been a couple of days, Mona was starting to grow on me. "Maybe she's not that bad," I thought.

Roni J.

A Daughters Rage

Jake

I laid on the 2-inch thick mattress that was thrown across the cold cot in the holding cell. I was sick to my stomach and refused to eat anything. I couldn't shake the thoughts that I was having. Not only was my wife dead and I was accused for the murder, but my gay lover had committed the actual crime with the help of another cop. But who was the question? Then I thought about Armando and the threats that he had made because I was dragging my ass with finding Mona. The whole situation had gotten out of control. I knew that my living or dying depended on the information I knew. I thought back to the day that I got caught up with Armando. It was late night on a Friday and I had been driving around the hood all day fucking with lil niggas and taking their money. I turned down Linwood Ave and come out a side alley when I heard a loud gunshot. I wasn't sure where it came from so I kept it moving until I saw a black Cadillac shoot passed me flying down Harford Rd. Turning on the police sirens and flashing lights, I took off behind the black Cadillac. I lived for police chases. "Show time," I yelled laughing. I didn't bother to call for backup. I didn't feel that I needed it. I was known in the streets as "Hulk" and nobody played with or fucked with me. I stood six feet five inches tall. I had a shiny bald head and my body was tight and ripped. I was tatted all over. I even had a pair of angel wings tatted on my back and light hazel brown eyes. All in all I was a sexy motherfucker and I knew it. Right as I was coming up on the tail end of the Caddie a dark blue Escalade ran into the back of me. Not hard enough to cause any real harm or damage but enough to slow me down. Pulling off to the side with the Escalade right behind me I was heated and ready to shoot the motherfucker who had just hit me. Stepping out of the squad car gun in hand, I walked up to the driver's side of the truck tapping on the window with my gun. "Roll dis bitch down before I shoot it down," I yelled but when the window came down all I saw was the barrel of a shiny all chrome Desert Eagle pointed in my face. "Get the fuck in nigga," was all I heard. I didn't know what to do.

I had done so many people dirty and thought I was getting my karma at that moment. So like a real nigga I accepted it and got in the truck. Once in I saw Armando in the passenger seat and Ray Ramirez in the back. I knew who Ray was but

A Daughters Rage

had no clue who Armando was. "This is what you're going to do because you have no choice," Ray said with a straight face and that was two years ago. Now I knew I had big problems because Armando and his crew were coldblooded killers and even though I wasn't scared, I knew that it was a matter of life or death. Going up against the Ramirez family was something I most definitely wasn't ready for but I was confident in myself and my crew.

Roni J.

A Daughters Rage

Mona

I knew I should've just listened to Heads and not gone searching for shit but Mya was not herself and I didn't like the vibe I was getting. Looking over at Mya and realizing she was asleep; I went into her bag and got her phone. I had to know what nigga that bitch was trying to keep from me. Scrolling through her text messages, I spotted a message ending with a smiley face. The number wasn't stored under a name so I quickly studied the number storing it in my mental database. After putting Mya's phone back in her bag, I got in bed beside her. I turned to face forward looking at my friend's back. "Bitch you're hiding something and I will find out what. If you think I'm playing don't believe me, and just watch," I thought. Then I tried my best to go to sleep.

Roni J.

A Daughters Rage

Heads

I sat on the side of my bed thinking about the situation I had gotten myself into. "I really hope I don't have to kill this nigga," I thought. Reaching into my nightstand drawer, I pulled out my meds. I opened the bottle and took one out. Popping the pill in my mouth without any water, I swallowed. "I wonder what my lil man doing," I thought about my son. I missed him a lot and lately I hadn't been spending much time with him. That shit with shorty was going to have to wait. I was going to see my son in the morning after I take her to Ray's grave site. I got undressed leaving on my tank top and boxers. I laid back on my bed and fell asleep.

Roni J.

A Daughters Rage

Armando's Warehouse

Santana came rushing into the warehouse sweating and angry. "How the fuck did she get out of here without you knowing Pops," he yelled. "Nigga I called you and asked you so how the fuck am I supposed to know," he yelled back. "All I know is I went to take a shit and when I went in and looked in the freezer the bitch was gone," Armando said while reaching for his cell that was ringing on the desk. Seeing who the number belonged to he immediately got nervous. "Hola," he answered. "I've got that bitch and I'm taking her with me. You've had more than enough time," the caller said before hanging up. Armando looked at Santana and yelled, "Let's go!" They barely made it out before the whole warehouse blew up throwing them both into the air.

Roni J.

A Daughters Rage

Mona

The next morning I woke up with the same attitude I had gone to sleep with. I didn't cook breakfast which Heads was looking forward to. I hadn't said much of anything to Mya either. "What's up Monie? You on your period?" Mya asked walking into the bathroom while I brushed my teeth.

"Look I'm not in a good mood right now and I don't have shit to say. So you can just call your nigga and talk to him," I said with an attitude. Mya didn't bother to respond. She walked off going to get her phone. She planned on doing exactly what Monie said. She reached in her bag and grabbed her phone. She powered it on; scrolled to the number she was looking for, and sent a text that said, "I may need you to find a way to come get me because this bitch is testing the waters." She ended the text with an angry face.

I walked out of the bathroom and into the kitchen where Heads was. He was eating a bowl of Maple brown sugar oatmeal. I smiled because I knew he was being smart because I didn't cook breakfast. "You need to get dressed. I'm going take you to your father's grave site first," he said. "Ok cool," I replied.

I walked back in the room and slipped on some baggy sweats and a big tee that Heads had given me. I grabbed my pink and white retro Jordan's that Mya had brought to me. "I'm about to ride out. Heads is taking me to my father's grave site," I said to Mya with a slight attitude. "Oh ok," was all Mya said. "Yeah this bitch is definitely up to something," I thought. Any other time that bitch was on my ass following me like a shadow. I grabbed my coat and left out of the room. When I walked into the living room, Heads was already standing by the door waiting. "You ready?" he asked. It would be his first time going to the grave site since the funeral. "Yes I'm as ready as I'll ever be," I said. He opened the door and we both walked out. "What's up with shorty? She not going?" he asked. "Naw I don't need her to go I'm good," I said. He nodded his head. Unlocking the car door and walking around to the passenger side, he opened the door for me. After I got in, he walked around to his side and got in as well. Using his remote to open the garage door. He waited for the door to open all the way before backing out. He backed out and used the remote to close the door. Then he pulled off. I rode in silence and it surprised Heads because he was sure that I would have a lot to say. He didn't ask questions he just drove while I looked out the window.

Back at the house, Mya was on her phone. "Yeah I'm tired of this shit babe," she yelled into the phone. I haven't even mentioned the money to her because she's a smart bitch. She's already on to my ass asking me a bunch of questions and shit," Mya said with an attitude. "Well she should because your ass is a snake. I can't wait until she finds out that your ass has been helping the enemy," Lo said laughing. "Shut the fuck up," Mya yelled. "You didn't have to make her suck your dick with my period blood dried up on it!" She busted out laughing. "I know that was some shit wasn't it," Lo said laughing as well. "Well look I'm going to go and see what I can find in this nigga's room and I'll call you back," Mya said hanging up. She didn't know how long they were going to be so she didn't have a lot of time.

About 45 minutes had passed we finally reached King Memorial Park. I was a little hesitant at first but I quickly got over it. "I just need a little time alone," I said looking at Heads. "Ok I'm going back to the car. I need to make a few phone calls," he said walking off. Once I couldn't see him anymore I began talking to my father. "Daddy why did you leave me?" I spoke aloud. "I can't do this anymore. Sandy is a ratchet hoe ass bitch! She doesn't love me and she doesn't give a fuck about me. All she does is beat me! I'm a hoe too Daddy! That's right I'm a hoe. I fuck for money! I have to that's how I've been surviving Daddy. Lo kidnapped me and made me suck his dick. For the last few days, I've been staying with Heads. He's been really nice to me. Uncle Santana and Papa Armando have Sandy. I'm just lost and scared Daddy. I need you and I miss you!" I bent down, kissed my father's tombstone, and got up to leave. Before I walked away, I turned and said, "I love you Papa."

"Love you too," I heard a voice say but when I turned around no one was there. I shook my head. "I'm really fucking tripping," I thought. I walked back to the car. I saw that Heads was on his phone so I decided to wait before I got in. I stood there looking around the graveyard. Heads tapped on the window for me to get in. I opened the door and got in. I didn't want to tell him that I heard my father's voice because he would think I was crazy. I

A Daughters Rage

looked at him and said, "Let's go get this crazy motherfucker!" He nodded and pulled off.

Roni J.

A Daughters Rage

About The Author

Born and raised in Baltimore, Maryland Authoress Roni J. has spent the last 12 years in the security field.

Roni J. started writing poems and short stories at the tender age of 12. An avid reader, Roni J was motivated to become an author herself. She is signed to Blaque Diamond Publications and is excited to have the opportunity to share her skills with the world. Roni J. has dreams of becoming a bestselling author.

Roni J has three children whom she adores and she often refers to as her world. Her hobbies are being a mom, reading, writing, cooking and helping others any way she can.

Roni J.

A Daughters Rage

Currently Available from Blaque Diamond Publications

Tales Of A Plus Size Diva: Lillian's Story by Shuantrell Perry

Justifiable Insanity by Authoress Juawel

Coming Soon from Blaque Diamond Publications

Giving Him Something He Can Feel by Damenia Uvonda

Mocha: The Ultimate Sacrifice by Authoress Meka

Tangled Intimacy: Iona's Story by Authoress Skyy Terrell

Diary Of A Hood Princess by Authoress K.L. Hall

Taste Like Kandi by Keita B

Man Thief by Cinnamon Brown

The Moscato Diaries by Fanita Moon Pendleton

Roni J.

If you have a manuscript you would like us to review

email us at
Blaquediamondpublications@gmail.com

CPSIA information can be obtained at www.ICGtesting.com
Printed in the USA
LVOW13s1544110714

393952LV00015B/603/P